Praise for
MRS. SMITH'S SPY SCHOOL FOR GIRLS

"Middle-grade readers of Stuart Gibbs's *Spy School*
as well as fans of boarding school adventures such as
Shannon Hale's *Princess Academy* will appreciate this
comical and exhilarating escapade."
—*School Library Journal*

"A sassy, new spy series with a spunky heroine,
multitalented sidekicks, and tense, rapid-fire adventure."
—*Kirkus Reviews*

"A fast-moving, twist-filled addition to the kid spy genre,
which builds to a nail-biter of a conclusion."
—*Publishers Weekly*

"An action-filled romp . . . Abigail's entertaining
narration tempers suspense with levity, and readers will
have a blast accompanying her through sticky situations."
—*Booklist*

Praise for
POWER PLAY

"A celebration of friendship and girl power, this exciting spy story will keep readers on the edge of their seats."
—*School Library Journal*

"Fearless wannabe spy Abby's return in her latest fast-paced, intriguing, international escapade involving a complex computer game guarantees a rousing read."
—*Kirkus Reviews*

Also by Beth McMullen

MRS. SMITH'S SPY SCHOOL FOR GIRLS
POWER PLAY

MRS. SMITH'S SPY SCHOOL
◄◄ FOR GIRLS ►►

Double Cross

Beth McMullen

ALADDIN

New York   London   Toronto   Sydney   New Delhi

This book is a work of fiction. Any references to historical events, real people, or real places are used fictitiously. Other names, characters, places, and events are products of the author's imagination, and any resemblance to actual events or places or persons, living or dead, is entirely coincidental.

🦢 ALADDIN

An imprint of Simon & Schuster Children's Publishing Division
1230 Avenue of the Americas, New York, New York 10020
First Aladdin paperback edition July 2020
Text copyright © 2019 by Beth McMullen
Cover illustration copyright © 2019 by Vivienne To
Also available in an Aladdin hardcover edition.
All rights reserved, including the right of reproduction in whole or in part in any form.
ALADDIN and related logo are registered trademarks of Simon & Schuster, Inc.
For information about special discounts for bulk purchases,
please contact Simon & Schuster Special Sales at 1-866-506-1949
or business@simonandschuster.com.
The Simon & Schuster Speakers Bureau can bring authors to your live event. For more information or to book an event contact the Simon & Schuster Speakers Bureau at 1-866-248-3049 or visit our website at www.simonspeakers.com.
Book designed by Laura Lyn DiSiena
The text of this book was set in Chaparral Pro.
Manufactured in the United States of America 0620 OFF
10 9 8 7 6 5 4 3 2 1
The Library of Congress has cataloged the hardcover edition as follows:
Names: McMullen, Beth, 1969– author.
Title: Double cross / by Beth McMullen.
Description: First Aladdin hardcover edition. | New York : Aladdin, 2019. |
Series: Mrs. Smith's Spy School for Girls ; [3] | Summary: While participating in the Challenge at Briar Academy, Abby and friends learn that their nemesis is using Briar as headquarters for planning an attack, and that the Ghost has inside help.
Identifiers: LCCN 2019001638 (print) | LCCN 2019002779 (eBook) |
ISBN 9781481490283 (eBook) | ISBN 9781481490269 (hardcover)
Subjects: | CYAC: Spies—Fiction. | Boarding schools—Fiction. | Schools—Fiction. | Friendship—Fiction. | Adventure and adventurers—Fiction. | BISAC: JUVENILE FICTION / Action & Adventure / General. | JUVENILE FICTION / Social Issues / New Experience. | JUVENILE FICTION / Girls & Women.
Classification: LCC PZ7.1.M4644 (eBook) | LCC PZ7.1.M4644 Dou 2019 (print) |
DDC [Fic]—dc23
LC record available at https://lccn.loc.gov/2019001638
ISBN 9781481490276 (paperback)

For my mother, Eva Von Ancken, for giving
me a lifelong love of books

Chapter 1

SAVING THE WORLD IS NO EXCUSE.

IF YOU WANT TO BE A SPY, and possibly save the world, you have to practice. Take advantage of every opportunity to improve your skills. Me and my best friends, Charlotte and Izumi, are serious about spying, which is why we've spent the last month of summer on the Smith School for Children campus perfecting a karate move we call Deadhead the Rose, where we roundhouse kick the withered flowers from their stems to make way for new blooms. As a gardening technique, it is much faster than pruning shears. We've gotten pretty good. I can deadhead an entire rosebush in under a minute.

We're kicking roses outside Headmaster Smith's office

window, in New England heat so unrelenting Charlotte keeps pretending to faint just to get a break, when Izumi whispers, "You guys. Come here."

We peel off our gardening gloves and squeeze in tight next to Izumi under the window, wide-open in hopes of catching a passing breeze. The air is a thick, humid blanket we cannot throw off. Staying low, we peer over the window ledge. Inside, Mrs. Smith alternately studies a piece of paper and fans herself with it. These original Smith School buildings have no air conditioning. Global warming is now in a race with tradition to see who breaks first. Mrs. Smith wears a headset and her resting expression, which is total annoyance.

"It's not without precedent," she says into the headset. "I started with the spy school well before sixteen, as did others. If I want to let this girl in early, I'll do it. She could be our next Veronica Brooks. She has a brilliant mind. We don't want to lose students who are truly *exceptional*."

Everyone knows Veronica Brooks is the gold standard in spying, but who is the other girl Mrs. Smith is talking about? There's a pause in the conversation. Izumi elbows me, eyes wide.

"I'm not *asking* you," Mrs. Smith continues. "I'm *informing* you. As a courtesy. Now, you have a lovely day."

She tosses the headset on her desk in a way that leaves

the *lovely day* sentiment in doubt. We crawl away from the window on our hands and knees, to a safe distance, and all begin talking at once.

"Is it us?" I whisper. *Me? Is she finally going to let me into the spy school?*

Before this gets really confusing, an explanation. The Smith School for Children is exactly as it sounds: a preppy paradise of redbrick buildings, climbing ivy and students in uncomfortable uniforms. We have a Latin school motto, which loosely translates to "don't be a jerk," and a coat of arms featuring a roaring lion (not kidding). Our hallways are lined with portraits of former headmasters, none of whom look like they can take a joke.

But get closer. Go deeper. Look underneath the school. And I don't mean that metaphorically. Below the buildings in the old tunnels and passageways, the Center hides the spy school, a secret training facility for teenage girl spies, kids who are innocent-looking on the outside but sharp on the inside. These are the girls getting done what the adults cannot. Because, after all, who suspects a kid? Unless we are noisy or badly behaved, we are invisible. We can move through the world without warranting so much as a second glance. By the time you realize the Center spies have come for you, it's too late.

Mrs. Smith was a founding member of the spy school. As was my mother, Jennifer Hunter. Yes. My mother was a spy. *Is* a spy? Being as I didn't find out until I was twelve, and then only by accident, I'm still a bit fuzzy on the details. Right now I could not tell you where Jennifer is or what she is doing. At home in our tiny New York City apartment reading the latest Stephen King or apprehending a notorious arms smuggler in Yemen? Your guess is as good as mine. A proper teenager would rebel against all this spy nonsense and possibly choose a life of crime just to spite her spy mom. But I'm not ordinary. I want in on the spy gig. Badly.

Alas, spying is only for those sixteen and older, which means too bad for me, despite having saved the world *twice* on behalf of the Center. But this new evidence suggests that Mrs. Smith might have changed her mind about the age limit.

"We need to get in that office," says Charlotte. "As in right now."

Izumi puts her hand on Charlotte's shoulder. "Is this a good idea?" she asks. "I mean, the whole reason we're here working the grounds during vacation is because we're being punished. Remember?"

Oh. Right. True. A few months ago, a disgruntled ex–Smith School student named Zachary Hazard tried to take over the world. We had to stop him. I'll admit we didn't follow our orders *exactly*, but the situation called for immediate action. Who knew that saving civilization as we know it was not a good enough excuse for breaking the rules?

"How could I forget?" Charlotte replies.

"But you don't care," Izumi says flatly.

"She cares a lot," I say.

Charlotte grins. "I do. So *much*. About who Mrs. Smith was talking about."

"We're going to spend the rest of our lives cleaning this campus," Izumi mutters.

We crawl back to the window and glance inside, making sure Mrs. Smith is gone. "Boost me up," I whisper. Izumi and Charlotte give me a shove over the window ledge. I fall headfirst into Mrs. Smith's office and freeze. What if she comes back? I can't very well say I'm pruning her desk fern. Quickly, I swipe the paper and throw myself back out the window. I have a lot of experience throwing myself from windows, so this is no big deal. The mound of decapitated rose heads cushions my landing. "Got it!"

We dash to the gazebo next to the Cavanaugh Family Meditative Pond and Fountain. It has shade, and if we sit in the corner we get a little bit of spray from the fountain.

Desperate times. Sweat drips from my forehead, making damp splotches on the paper.

"What does it say?" Charlotte asks, wedging in for a better view. I stink like mulch, and yet she manages to smell like rose petals. How does she do that? Izumi lies flat on the gazebo brick floor, blowing her straight dark bangs out of her eyes.

The girl on the paper is not me. Or any of us. That's bad. What makes it infinitely worse is whose name *is* on the paper.

Poppy Parsons.

Chapter 2

SMARTS. WITS. PRESSURE.

POPPY PARSONS *IS* EXCEPTIONAL, and she is the first one to say so. She speaks five languages, builds computers in her spare time, is nationally ranked in Fortnite, and runs the school's Dungeons and Dragons club (with an iron fist, apparently). She can run the mile in six minutes flat, is a black belt in karate, has an enviable cascade of honey-blond curls and a cute British accent, and once filed a complaint about me with the student disciplinary committee regarding the improper composting of an apple core. Needless to say, Poppy and I are *not* friends.

Izumi says Poppy has self-esteem issues, and that's why she talks constantly about her own awesomeness. She is really trying to convince *herself* that she is okay. This does not help me feel better about her name being on that paper rather than mine.

But I do feel pretty good about my new muscles, compliments of long hours of gardening, painting, scrubbing, and perfecting Deadhead the Rose. I have never been so strong in my life. When I see Toby on move-in day, I lift him clear off the ground to demonstrate. Toby is my other best friend, although different from Charlotte and Izumi.

"Put me down!" Toby howls, so I drop him like a sack of flour. He doesn't like that, either. "What is wrong with you?"

"I've spent a lot of time outdoors," I say, flexing an impressive bicep.

"Whatever." Suitcases and a big steamer trunk surround Toby. The lobby overflows with returning students and frazzled parents, all twirling in different directions. The headmaster's welcome-back lunch happens in an hour, but from the looks of this mess, everyone is going to be late.

"Abby!" Drexel Caine, Toby's dad and my biggest fan, hugs me so hard, I gasp.

"Drexel, let her go," Toby says with obvious disgust. Here at Smith we call our parents by their first names, just to annoy them. But Drexel seems downright tickled. He grins at Toby and tousles his hair like he's off to kinder-garten. "Son, I just love you guys. That's all."

Man, this is bad. Drexel has been lobotomized by hap-piness and second chances. Until last year, he was the poster parent for benign neglect. He forgot Toby's birth-day. He pulled a no-show on Parents' Weekend. He never made it to a single basketball game. He was too busy being the genius behind DrexCon to be bothered.

But when Zachary Hazard kidnapped him and he almost died, everything changed. Now he drinks his coffee from a WORLD'S #1 DAD! mug. Poor Toby. It's like a code-red emergency. Attentive parents can be a nightmare. Believe me, I *know*.

"Guess what?" Drexel rubs his hands together like a kid on Christmas morning about to dive into a mountain of presents. His eyes shine. "Tell her, Toby. Tell her!"

"Drexel," Toby hisses, but this does little. Drexel is per-manently thrilled by everything.

"Okay, I'll tell her," he says, practically jumping up and down. "DrexCon is sponsoring the Invitational Interschool Global Problems and Solutions Challenge this year. Isn't that the *best*?"

Wow, he really has gone off the deep end. The Invitational Interschool Global Problems and Solutions Challenge, or the

Challenge, as we call it, because its full name is just plain ridiculous, was started fifty years ago by Emma and Gemma Glass. As Jennifer likes to say, there's more than one way to save the world, and Emma and Gemma believed children should be encouraged to apply their classroom smarts to solving the many problems humans face, things like how to make sure everyone has enough food and clean water, a safe place to live, and an education. We come from so much privilege, the sisters said, don't we have an obligation to help those with less?

The Challenge was their answer, a biennial competition where teams of students perform three tasks around a theme: providing clean water, increasing the food supply, preventing wars, limiting pollution and creating clean energy, curing disease, recycling waste, and so on. The tasks test your smarts, your wits, and how well you perform under pressure. Smarts. Wits. Pressure.

To get invited, you have to have done something cool, like invent a garbage-eating robotic shark or figure out cheap travel to Mars or mastermind a peace process for the Middle East. Winners get full-on glory—international recognition and a pass to brag about being the best *forever*.

"Push kids out of their comfort zone," Emma said, "and they will surprise you." Or maybe it was Gemma? Anyway, I'm not surprised DrexCon is sponsoring this year's Challenge. Now that Drexel is in love with the world, he wants to make it better.

"That's exciting," I say, nudging Toby in the ribs. He ignores me.

"Smarts, wits, and pressure," Drexel says with a grin. "These kids that get invited are truly exceptional. I've missed so much!"

Back up a second. Did he say "exceptional"?

"And," Drexel continues, grinning, "I suggested Headmaster Smith send you four as a *team*. I have some influence as the lead sponsor." He winks conspiratorially. "I told the organizers all about that Cookie app you were working on this summer. How great am I?"

Toby goes pale. "Tell me you didn't. I don't *want* to do the Challenge."

"I did! And you do! I want the world to know how amazing you are! Of course, Mrs. Smith needs to approve, but I don't see that as a problem. Now why don't you two run along and get caught up? I'll get your stuff moved in, Tobes."

Tobes? This might be worse than I thought. As soon as we are out of earshot, Toby grabs my shoulders.

"I can't go on like this," he says, face tight with distress, curly black hair in a wild halo around his head. "He wants to hang out *all* the time. He makes me pancakes in animal shapes with chocolate chip eyeballs. He bought us *matching* baseball gloves."

"He calls you Tobes," I add.

"I'm losing my mind. You have no idea."

"Hey, remember my mother was headmaster last year. I know what it's like being under a microscope." We weave through a bunch of incoming Lower Middles, confused and scared, standing by parents who are also confused and scared. Nothing like boarding school drop-off day to make emotions run high.

"So where *is* Teflon, anyway?" Toby asks. Teflon is my mother's spy code name. I wish I were kidding.

"I don't know," I say. "Bulgaria? Romania? Beijing? The Himalayas? Back home in our apartment? If you're such a fan, why don't *you* keep track of her?"

Toby holds up his hands. "Okay. Got it. Don't ask about Teflon." We exit Main Hall and walk along the path toward McKinsey House dormitory, where I live.

"What's the Cookie app?" I ask.

"A failure, that's what," Toby snaps. "I can't believe Drexel told people about it! Basically, I spent all summer trying to figure out how to send a smell through a phone— you know, like attached to a text or something."

"Like stinky socks?" I ask.

"No! Like cookies or, I don't know, kittens."

"Kittens don't smell," I point out.

"You know what I mean," he growls. "Good things. Happy things. Jeez, what's wrong with wanting to spread a little happiness?"

"Nothing! What happened?"

"It didn't work," he grumbles. "I kept on practically poisoning myself. The cookie smell was toxic. I even barfed once."

"I'm sorry," I say. "I'm glad you're okay. Do you really think Drexel will get us invited to the Challenge?"

"Oh, I'm sure of it," Toby says with a grimace. "I mean, this is *Drexel Caine* we're talking about, even if version 2.0 is practically unrecognizable. For the record, we are *not* going to the Challenge. Everyone here already thinks I'm favored because of him."

And everyone is right. The new science and technology building is, after all, Caine Hall.

Dozens of girls buzz around McKinsey House in a state of move-in disarray. Izumi and Charlotte sit on a bench opposite the dorm and critically survey the chaos.

"You'd think after a hundred years," offers Charlotte, "they'd come up with a better way to move seven hundred and fifty-four students into their dorms at the same time."

"You'd think," concurs Izumi.

"Look who I found," I say.

"Welcome back, Toby," Charlotte says, grinning. "Where's Drexel?"

"Please, let's not talk about him."

"Oh, come on," says Izumi. "It's nice that your dad wants to spend time with you."

"All the time," I say. "*Every* day."

"Parents," Charlotte says with a shrug. "What are you going to do?"

While my mom is a superspy, Izumi's mom is the United States ambassador to Japan, and Charlotte's dad is richer than the entire country of Norway. At least none of them are boring. Toby plops down on the bench. Charlotte regales him with stories about our summer planting rose-bushes and driving tractors around on the soccer field, but my mind is stuck on Drexel, the Challenge, and "exceptional."

"Did Abby tell you about Poppy?" Izumi asks. "The one who gets to be part of the spy school *before* she's sixteen?"

Toby narrows his gaze. "Poppy Parsons? In spy school? Like, *now*?" Before I came along and messed things up, Toby was Mrs. Smith's right-hand kid for spy gadgets. Now he has to wait until he's sixteen too.

"We overheard Mrs. Smith talking about it," Izumi clarifies. "Exceptions can be made for *exceptional* candidates. Like Veronica before and Poppy Parsons now."

Toby gets a moony look on his face whenever the name Veronica is mentioned. Veronica Brooks is a former Smith School superspy who begrudgingly trained me last year when Mrs. Smith wanted to use me as bait to find my missing mother. Veronica is also the object of Toby's unrequited affection.

We sit in silence for a minute, contemplating the great unfairness of Poppy Parsons. She has never once saved the world, at least not that we know of. She probably wouldn't even know where to start. What do we have to do to prove our worth?

And that's when it hits me. If being exceptional gets us into the spy school early, we have to prove our exceptionalness, and everyone knows the Challenge is where that is done. Challenge winners simply cannot be ignored. Sure, our chances of actually winning are slim, but can't we at least *try*? Now all I have to do is convince my friends that going is the most brilliant idea since electricity, since the Internet, since, I don't know, Fortnite!

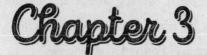

Chapter 3

NORMAL IS BORING.

"I'M IN!" YELPS CHARLOTTE after I pitch the idea. "We have smarts, we *definitely* have wits, and I happen to think we are *very* good under pressure."

"Count me in," adds Izumi. "This will make my mother super happy. It might even be *fun*."

"Worst. Idea. Ever," says Toby flatly. "And not fun. Definitely not fun."

"Come on, Toby," I respond. "You don't mean that."

"I do," he says. "I mean it. I mean it a lot."

"Please?" I beg.

"No," Toby says.

"Pretty please?"

"No," he repeats.

"So you'll think about it?" I ask.

"Don't be boring," adds Charlotte.

"And dull," says Izumi.

"What's wrong with just being a nice, normal, regular, boring Smith School student?" Toby grumbles. "Go to class. Mess with my computers. Hang out at the Annex and eat cheese fries. I've been on the Smith campus for all of an hour, and already you're trying to ruin it."

Clearly, a chance at getting into the spy school early is not incentive enough. I need another approach. "Wouldn't it be cool to tell *Veronica* you won the Challenge?" I suggest. "She won her senior year, remember?"

Toby visibly perks up. "You think she'd care?"

"Absolutely," I say. "These things matter to Veronica. It would give you heaps to talk about the next time you see each other. Compare notes, go over winning strategies. She might even call you to say congratulations. You know she monitors these things." I don't know if that is exactly true, but I can totally see her doing it. It fits with her personality.

Toby is quiet, considering.

"Think about it this way," Charlotte offers. "We'd get out of Smith for a week. Different disgusting cafeteria food. No math class with Wacky Mr. Warren. No school meeting."

"We can check out another campus," I say. "Maybe it will be horrible and we'll come back to Smith all grateful and stuff."

Izumi bursts out laughing. "As if. Where is the Challenge this year, anyway?"

"Briar Academy," Toby says. "On the other side of Hartford."

"Fabulous!" I shout. "I love Hartford this time of year!"

Toby stares at a gaggle of new girls trying to defy physics and cram a too-big box through the front door of McKinsey House. They try it a number of different ways, and even though it is never going to fit, they keep at it. Determined or foolish? Sometimes it's a fine line. We wait patiently as Toby turns the possibilities over in his head.

"Okay," he says finally. "I'll do it. But on one condition."

"Anything," I say.

"You have to tell me who Iceman is."

Well, there goes *that* brilliant idea. Iceman is the world's most notorious black hat, a hacker of epic reputation. Nothing is safe from Iceman. Last year, we discovered she's not much older than we are and has *everyone* fooled. She helped us when she didn't have to, and we owe it to her to keep her identity secret.

"No," we say together.

His eyes turn steely. "Fine. If we go, I want to *win*. Winning means I'm Veronica's equal." Of course, we laugh hysterically at this while Toby waits patiently for us to stop. "You know what I mean. She'll have to take me seriously. She might even want to hang out and talk about our Challenge victory win. Got it?"

We all have individual skills and talents, but as a team they add up to something bigger and better. Everyone knows that Toby is a master of invention. No one would be surprised to see him win the Challenge. Izumi is a star athlete, takes math with the seniors, and can logic her way out of anything. Charlotte can learn a new language in a week, give or take, plus she has the uncanny ability to manipulate people without them even knowing it's happening. In truth, our team is pretty close to my definition of "exceptional" already.

Except for me. What do I bring to the table? This thought is much too alarming for move-in day, so I push it aside. We squish Toby in a group hug that he very vocally hates. We are going to the Challenge! We will *prove* our worth! We will get into spy school early!

But that night, as we huddle on the floor of Izumi's dormitory room, a box of pizza between us, scrutinizing our new class schedules and teachers, I can't get it out of my mind. What am I good at? I want to ask my friends, but what if they don't have an answer? What if everyone realizes I'm dead weight, a fraud, an impostor, of no help to our team?

I take this discomfort to bed with me. I toss and turn for a while, and just as I might actually fall asleep, my mother calls. I know it's her because my phone indicates the caller cannot be identified. Also, she keeps odd hours.

I can tell right away that Jennifer is not in our New York City apartment. There's wind in the background and the sound of crashing waves.

"Don't ask," she says, before even a "hello."

"Got it," I say.

"How was move-in day? I'm sorry I wasn't there to help you."

"I moved in a month ago," I say. "Remember?"

"Right! Yes. Of course. I hear Drexel got you invited to the Challenge."

My mother is probably in the middle of the ocean, and she *still* knows what's happening before I do. With Jennifer, even a measure of privacy is a dream. I could drill her on her sources, but she will never tell. She's not a legend for nothing.

"Yes," I mutter.

"Congratulations. I happen to believe you four will make an excellent team." There's a loud crash in the background and shouting, definitely not in a language I understand. "Hold on."

My mother covers the receiver and joins the shouting. Thirty seconds later, she's back. "Boy, some people just don't understand the most basic instructions. Modern-day pirates have a lot to learn. Now, where were we? The Challenge?"

Did she say "pirates"? "It doesn't matter," I mumble. "We can't win with me on the team. I'm not interesting enough."

"What on earth does that mean?" The shouting in the background grows faint. A door slams. Footsteps echo on a hard surface. "You can't seriously think that's true."

"But what makes me special?" I blurt. "What am I good at?"

"Abigail Hunter," Jennifer says sternly. "You are loyal and kind and determined and fearless, and you do not quit. Especially when things get tough." My ears grow warm. "Now, it's one thing for me to say you are all those things. But it is quite another for you to believe them about yourself. You don't need a spy school to be special. Or a Challenge, for that matter. Do you understand?"

Maybe I don't need those things, but I *want* them. Before I can respond, the background yelling resumes. Did I hear the word "sinking"? "Oh, boy. Gotta go, honey. But don't worry. Everything is fine! Have a great first day of classes!"

And just like that, she's gone.

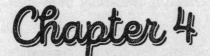

Chapter 4

TIES OF TORTURE.

EVERY WEDNESDAY MORNING, we have school meeting, a ritualistic torture during which the entire Smith School student body is crammed into the Main Hall auditorium to listen to twenty minutes of announcements (Join synchronized swimming! Come out for the debate club! Lost and found has forty-eight Smith hoodies already!) and a minilecture on a motivational topic (Integrity! Duty! Empathy!). Intentional absence from school meeting means demerits. If a student incurs enough demerits, she will spend her weekend cleaning toilets or sorting dirty uniforms in the athletic center. Neither option is particularly appealing. Most students spend school meeting perfecting the art of open-eyed napping.

The heat has not let up, and our ugly uniform skirts and shirts don't help. To make matters worse, Mrs. Smith, rehabilitated and returned to the helm of the Smith School asylum at the end of the last school year, has instituted an addition to our wretched uniforms—the *tie*. For girls, it's a limp piece of red ribbon that slides around our collars and loops into a bow. For the boys, it's a traditional tie, but from the looks of my classmates streaming toward the auditorium, 90 percent of them didn't finish watching the YouTube video on how to tie a proper Windsor knot before school meeting. We are a ragtag, wilted bunch.

Toby falls in with us. "Hey, guys," he says with a yawn. His tie is askew, and there is cat hair all over his pants. Is he harboring a secret pet in his dorm room? I wouldn't put it past him. If Toby asked, Drexel would install a private petting zoo in the hallway. What are the chances the cat's name is Veronica? He pulls a shiny rose-gold phone from his pocket and uses it to examine his teeth, making sure his breakfast isn't lodged in there. It's not, but I don't care about that.

"Is that what I think it is?" I whisper, eyes glued to the gold phone.

"If you think it's my phone, then yes."

"You know what I mean. Is it a *spy* phone?" Spy phones do things that regular phones don't, like spray hot water in an enemy's face or blast a whistle that deafens all those around you. The idea of the spy phone is to create a distraction, buying time so you can escape a bad situation.

Toby glances anxiously over his shoulder. "It's *not* a spy phone," he says, yanking on his tie.

Seven hundred and fifty-four students, minus Nathan Winters, who suffers from school–meeting-related narcolepsy and never shows up, squeeze through the narrow doors of the auditorium. We take our assigned seats. By design, none of us sit near one another. As if we'd somehow cause an uprising in school meeting by mere proximity.

Mrs. Smith takes the stage. She isn't hot in her khaki suit, white blouse (no *tie*), and stiletto heels. It's possible that the real Mrs. Smith failed rehab and the Center replaced her with a robot. She scans the student body. We wiggle and squirm, baking in our stupid uniforms.

"My, you all look lovely this morning," she purrs. "For those of you questioning the addition to our standard uniform, we are simply paying homage to our past." Behind her the huge screen flashes a black-and-white photograph of a dorky Smith School student, circa 1958, wearing the terrible tie. "During my absence, some of you have become distracted from our core belief: *Non tamen ad reddet*. Not to take, but to give back. It is important to remember our roots, our foundations, our *purpose*."

Murmurs of displeasure ripple through the crowd. Adults always go on about the good old days, but in reality, they weren't always so good.

"Now I have some exciting news to share this morning," she continues. "As you all know, every two years we participate in the Invitational Interschool Global Problems and Solutions Challenge, an opportunity to showcase the overall high quality of the Smith student." It sounds like she's describing a steak. I glance down the row at Toby, who rolls his eyes and pretends to go to sleep.

"It is my job to recommend a team to represent our school, one that is best suited to creatively solving the problems that challenge the world today. At the last Challenge, we placed first, and I expect us to do so again. Join me, and let's congratulate our very own team of Owen Elliott Staar and Poppy Parsons, who will be headed to Briar Academy in one month's time to compete!"

My heart sinks. How can this be? Drexel built the science center! Down the aisle, Toby grins. There is a wave of muted grumbling from the roughly seven hundred students who wanted an invite. Smith is nothing if not competitive, and the Challenge is a big deal. To make matters worse, now we have to listen to Poppy gloat. She storms the stage as Owen Elliott dawdles behind. He's the only kid at Smith who can tolerate Poppy. We suspect he's too nice to tell her to go away. He's also the boy who hit me in the face with a squash ball last year and landed me in the infirmary with a black eye. He said it was an accident. He apologized no fewer than four hundred times. I thought it was because Jennifer was headmaster and he was worried about getting in trouble. But eventually I realized his regret was genuine.

As Owen Elliott and Poppy join Mrs. Smith onstage, I slump further in my chair. In my head, the plan had worked perfectly. We got in the Challenge, we won, we gracefully accepted offers of early admittance to the spy school. Of course, all my plans work in my head. It's when they meet reality that things go sideways.

"Poppy." Mrs. Smith swoons. "Would you like to share a few words of wisdom with your classmates?"

The distinct sound of gagging rises from the student body. Mrs. Smith glares. Did she insist on the ties so she could easily strangle us when we get out of line? Poppy elbows Owen Elliott out of the way, takes the microphone, and tosses her perfect hair dramatically. Owen Elliott scrutinizes his cuticles as his sole teammate delivers a speech on how to be awesome like she is.

"Here's the deal, fellow students. My dormitory is so loud I can barely hear myself think. And whenever I ask a girl to turn down her music or turn down her voice or turn off her lights, she will inevitably just blow me off, you know? Like, not listen *at all*, be totally rude. So I took action and designed Blackout, which is what got me invited to the Challenge. Blackout is a little bit of computer code that can infiltrate any of your electronics and turn down your music or turn off your laptop or even blow out your lights. And if you keep *yelling* all the time instead of using an indoor voice, I'll just shut off the power to your room entirely and you will be left in a blackout. If you can't behave, I'll do it for you. Get it?"

An eerie silence settles over the auditorium. Students throw one another sideways glances. Did she just say what I think she just said? Why, yes, she did. Poppy is prepared to infiltrate your dorm room and disrupt your life if you get on her nerves. No wonder she doesn't have friends. Owen Elliott looks set to collapse in horror. A low hiss moves through the crowd, but Poppy doesn't seem to notice. She had better wrap this up or things are going to get ugly. Mrs. Smith stands nearby, glowing with pride. What a pair.

"But maybe they invited me because of the smart cloth?" Poppy muses, spinning the microphone cord around her hand. The hissing grows louder. "It tells you if you're too hot or too cold or thirsty or whatever, all on an app. Get it?"

Isn't this why we have brains? I guess Poppy thinks our sad human heads could use some improvement. Finally, Mrs. Smith shows mercy and reclaims the microphone before there is a revolt.

"Isn't that so interesting?" Mrs. Smith asks, herding Poppy and Owen Elliott offstage. "We should all strive to be like these two. They will make us proud. Oh, and before I forget, there's a second team this year. Apparently." She pauses, crinkling up her nose with disgust, and I just *know* we're in.

After school meeting is adjourned, I rush out into the hallway to find my team. Instead, I end up elbow to elbow with Owen Elliott.

"Nice tie," he says with a grin. Owen is tall and skinny with unkempt brown hair and eyelashes like a giraffe's. His parents are divorced, and he spends summers in India, where his father lives.

"At least mine isn't held together with a rubber band," I say. Owen's hand floats to his neck.

"I was running late," he replies, rolling his eyes. "Are you guys really going to the Challenge?" His surprise does not please me.

"Do you have a problem with that?" I shoot back. He looks momentarily stung.

"No! I . . . just meant . . . congratulations." But his sentiments probably reflect what the general student body is thinking—we got in on something other than our merits. My cheeks flush.

"I bet we beat *you*," I snap. Being mean to Owen Elliott is like kicking a puppy. And yet here I am. His face registers my annoyance.

"I think you really have a shot," he says. And now he's being nice? What is *wrong* with this boy? I stomp away, feeling uncomfortably confused, leaving a bewildered Owen Elliott in my wake.

My friends huddle on the steps next to the bronze bust of Smith's founding father, Channing Smith. Channing has a wide forehead, small eyes, and a thick mane of hair. Oddly enough, in the portrait of Channing that hangs outside Mrs. Smith's office, he is bald save an unattractive fringe. Creative license? Currying favor? Or maybe, as Jennifer likes to say, the truth lies somewhere in the messy middle.

Izumi is so excited she bounces on her heels. "It's really happening! We're going to the Challenge!"

"It's cool," Charlotte agrees. "I hear Briar is way nice."

"There's so much work to do," Toby frets. "We need to research and study up on all the previous Challenges. See what they had to do. Come up with a plan. I should call Veronica. Get some tips. Right? Is that a good idea?"

It takes them a minute to notice I'm simmering. "What's with you?" Charlotte asks. "Isn't this what you wanted? Why aren't you happy?"

"I *am* happy," I shout. "But Owen Elliott is beyond annoying. The worst."

"The nicest kid in school? That Owen Elliott?"

"None other."

"Boy, he really gets under your skin," Izumi says.

"We're *already* getting a hard time for being selected," I say.

"Did he say that?" asks Charlotte. "Specifically?"

"Not exactly."

"What *did* he say?"

"Congratulations?" I respond meekly.

"I can totally see why you're so mad," Charlotte says, with a smirk.

Toby's eyes float to the space above my head. "Maybe go a little easy on him. His parents are, well, kind of jerks."

We fall silent. In this context, "jerk" can mean any number of things. They ignore him, they expect perfection, they helicopter, they intrude, they belittle, they trivialize, they demand. They use him against each other. They forget he is even there. None of it feels good.

"That stinks," says Izumi.

"It does," I agree.

"Either way," says Charlotte after a pause, "we're going to crush Team OP."

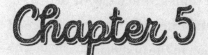

Chapter 5

OWEN ELLIOTT DOES WHAT?

BEING AS WE WERE HERE ON CAMPUS a month before everyone else, me, Izumi, and Charlotte have staked our claim to the McKinsey House common room. We lounge on the ugly plaid furniture, eat contraband Doritos, and obsess over the school's electronic bulletin board, affectionately nicknamed TrashTalk, where we are supposed to post things like *volleyball practice has been moved back a half hour* and *did anyone find a Smith School hoodie, size large, with a tear in the sleeve?* Instead, we use it to, well, trash-talk one another whenever possible. Currently, we are trending, which is almost always a bad thing. 55 percent of the school thinks we deserve to go to the Challenge, 35 percent thinks we don't, with 10 percent who could not care less and think the rest are a bunch of losers for having an opinion in the first place.

"Look," says Charlotte, holding up her phone. "It's Owen Elliott *defending* us against Tucker Harrington III." I quickly read the exchange, momentarily speechless that Tucker Harrington III, a big, dumb, obnoxious bully, can actually *spell* "cheaters." A fizzy, warm sensation fills my chest.

"Jeez, Abby, look at you," says Charlotte, grinning.

"What?" I demand.

"You totally *like* him," she says.

"Who?"

"Don't play dumb. And he likes you too. It's kind of sweet. And gross at the same time."

What is she talking about? Owen Elliott is a dork with big feet. Plus, he gave me a black eye. I definitely don't like him. I can barely tolerate him. And he certainly doesn't like me. Unacceptable.

"For the record," I growl, "I do *not* like him. And he does *not* like me. Have you noticed that's he's surgically attached to Poppy?"

"And you think *I'm* socially clueless," snorts Izumi.

"Well, you are," admits Charlotte. "But so is Abby. What would you guys do without me?"

I pelt her with a handful of chips. "Don't say Owen Elliott likes me, because . . . just . . . yuck. I refuse to accept it."

"You accepting it doesn't matter that much," Izumi says. Oh, no. She believes this nonsense too? Why do I feel so weird all of a sudden? He *hit* me in the face with a squash ball. That's it. Not thinking about Owen Elliott *any* more.

"I'm done with this conversation," I say.

"Good," says Izumi, "because we are due in Mrs. Smith's office in five minutes."

"Wait! Why?" I shout. Quickly, I inventory our activities since the start of school, and there is nothing suspect. We are on the straight and narrow, the epitome of the well-behaved Smith student.

"Oh, relax," says Charlotte. "She's just going to lecture us before we leave for the Challenge on codes of conduct and ask us not to embarrass Smith and blah, blah, blah."

I exhale sharply. A lecture. I can handle that.

It's almost October, and yet the heat won't let go. By the time we meet Toby in Main Hall, we're full-on sweating. Poppy and Owen Elliott are there too. We all look wilted.

"The competition," says Poppy, with an evil grin.

"Look," says Charlotte. "It's Team OP. Overpowered with no place to go."

"Charming as always," replies Poppy.

"Come on, guys," says Toby. "We shouldn't fight. Veronica says it's important for Smith teams to have each other's backs."

Poppy reels on Toby. "You've been quizzing past winners?" she asks hotly.

"No!" he responds. "We're friends! Sort of. Kind of? Never mind. All I'm saying is we're competing for the same school."

Poppy waves him off. "Maybe *you* are," she says. "But we're in it to win it, right, Owen Elliott?" Owen Elliott mutters something and stares at the floor.

Charlotte narrows her gaze on Poppy. "You know, TrashTalk favors us two to one." This is a total lie, but Charlotte delivers it with such confidence, Poppy blanches. Recovering quickly, she juts her chin out in defiance.

"TrashTalk is a waste of time and resources," she says. "Used primarily by people with low intelligence and a lack of imagination. And they will all be proved wrong once we get to Briar."

Charlotte isn't pleased with the implication that she is an idiot, but before it comes to blows, Mrs. Smith beckons us into her office. It's frosty inside. It could be the air-conditioning or Mrs. Smith's charming personality.

She reminds us we represent Smith and should act accordingly. We are to wear our uniforms, mind our manners, act civilly, and enjoy the spirit of competition. And remember, our reputation is on the line. In other words, there will be a price to pay for screwing up.

As we shuffle out of Mrs. Smith's office, Toby hangs back, a look of concern clouding his face. He can't back out now, can he?

"How was Veronica?" I ask, hoping to distract him.

"Good," he says. "Great, actually. She just won some award."

"For being the best at everything in the world?" I ask.

"Well, yeah." But the look stays on Toby's face.

"Okay, spill it," I say. "What's up?"

"I just wonder if this is a good idea," he says. What is he talking about? Life, the universe, spy school, math class?

"You are going to have to be more specific," I say.

"The Challenge," he replies. "Using it to get into spy school. Not doing it for what it's meant for. You know, bettering the world for humanity and stuff."

Uh-oh. This feels heavy. We sit down on a bench in empty Main Hall. "Explain," I urge.

"I want back into spy school as bad as anyone," he says quietly. "I mean, working with Veronica and Mrs. Smith before she kicked me out, it was the best. I felt, I don't know, like I had a purpose."

I'm paying close attention now, and I have no idea where this is going. "I get that," I respond.

"And we keep trying to get back in, and we keep getting further away. Do you know what I mean?" Sure. I've been on all the same misadventures he's been on. And it's true they have not endeared us to our headmaster. "What happens if we just play by the rules and wait until we are sixteen and then maybe get back into spy school like that? Like everyone else?"

Wait a minute. While Poppy Parsons goes off and saves the world, we sit around and eat cheese fries? I mean, eating cheese fries is not a bad thing, but really? I keep my mouth shut, pretty sure the thoughts in my head will not be helpful if I say them aloud.

"If we mess up again," Toby says gravely, "we may *never* get in. How far are you willing to go?"

As far as I have to, Toby. But I keep that in my head as well. "Let's just go to the Challenge and have fun and do our best. Maybe we'll get to build a bunch of battle drones and race them around campus. That would be cool, right?"

Toby's gaze tells me he's aware I've sidestepped the question. The hint of disappointment makes a tight spot in my chest. But as his look changes, I know he's letting it go.

"We need to win," he says, sticking a finger in my face so I know he's serious. "Remember, winning means a minimum of at least four conversations with Veronica. Maybe I can even work out a trip to spy college to debrief on our shared success."

I like the direction of this conversation much better. "You could form a club," I suggest. "The Smith School Global Challenge Winners Association. Membership of two. Unless you want us to join?"

"Um, no thank you." We walk down the hallway, bantering about Veronica and Toby's club, my chest slowly loosening.

Two days later, we're off to Briar Academy.

Chapter 6

THE BRIAR LUXURY RESORT— I MEAN SCHOOL.

THE FIRST THING WE DO UPON ARRIVAL at Briar Academy is ditch the uniforms and trash the ties in exchange for shorts and Smith School T-shirts. Only then can we fully take in our surroundings. Briar Academy sits in the middle of two hundred and fifty acres of Connecticut forest. If the Smith School for Children is fancy, Briar is completely over-the-top. Modern glass buildings are spread across a lush green campus woven with intricate English gardens, dotted with large sculptures and pieces of art. Smith is the expected mental image of boarding school. Briar is not.

We are assigned dorm rooms in a brand-new building

on the southern edge of campus. All the rooms are singles and include bathrooms with oversize Jacuzzi tubs. The towels are fluffy and soft.

"This lifestyle will make us weak," chides Izumi. I hate to admit it, but not having to share four grimy shower stalls with a thousand other girls is something I could get used to.

"We should transfer," says Charlotte.

Nestled into the campus is a lake complete with a family of paddling ducks and a dock with fancy boats for the rowing team. There is a private ski slope, a golf course, and an aquatic center, separate from the athletic facilities. There are twelve pristine soccer fields. It's possible I spy a planetarium.

Truly, this place makes Smith look like a dump. But it also feels unused, like it sprang fully formed from the ground just yesterday. The Briar school uniform is cargo pants and T-shirts, which makes us green with envy. We are assigned a minder to help us get oriented. Jane Ann has black hair down to her waist and fingernails painted bright orange. Toby cannot take his eyes off her.

"Congratulations on making the Challenge," Jane Ann gushes. She walks backward along the stone pathway so she can make eye contact as we move. It's one of those tricks tour guides practice. "We are *beyond* excited to host. It's a dream come true. I'm not competing myself, but I'm *so* grateful that I can help by being your guide. Go Briar!"

Talk about school spirit. I raise an eyebrow at Charlotte, who rolls her eyes. Our procession continues down the pathway, past a series of gleaming steel and glass buildings. No red brick or climbing ivy here. "We've seen a lot of big changes at Briar recently," Jane Ann says, as if reading from a script. "Two years ago, a new headmaster was installed, and he decided to change what Briar was all about. A full renovation followed. We're really lucky to have world-class facilities. The headmaster says soon *everyone* will know our name. Everyone will want to come here." Her grin threatens to swallow her face. It's boiling outside, and she doesn't sweat. She might be a cyborg.

Somewhere, a bell chimes, and the grounds flood with students hustling from class to class. They smile and laugh, waving at us, yelling congratulations. This is a happy place. *Abnormally* happy. Is it the Jacuzzi tubs? Maybe it's an army of cyborgs?

As if reading my mind, Jane Ann says, "The students are in a really good mood. We get Challenge week off, to watch the competitions and cheer everyone on." To our left is the library, the science center, and a theater designed to look like a slice of Broadway, complete with neon lights and a marquee advertising an upcoming production of *Hamlet*. We take a seat on some benches opposite the theater. Jane Ann stares at us expectantly. I feel we are already not living up to her expectations as Challenge participants. "Any questions about Briar?" she asks. "What else can I tell you about our crazy *awesome* school?"

"Do you know what the Challenge tasks are?" Charlotte replies.

Jane Ann visibly recoils. "Of course not," she says sternly. "The tasks remain under lock and key until they are announced to everyone at the same time. Otherwise, it would be unfair. It would be *cheating*. We don't cheat at Briar. It's against the honor code, and we take the code very seriously."

"Just asking," Charlotte says defensively.

"Briar is really nice," I offer as a distraction.

It works. Jane Ann grins. "We *love* it here. But I want to hear all about the *amazing* things you do at Smith! No one gets into the Challenge without being *amazing*." Her gaze is sharp. Maybe it's the heat, but I'm suddenly uncomfortable. She is not likely to be impressed by Deadhead the Rose. Izumi elbows me in the ribs. "Go ahead," she whispers. "Explain how we are amazing."

I can't very well tell Jane Ann how we saved the world from the Ghost, can I?

The Ghost is the world's ultimate baddy. Toby describes his empire as a giant wheel where each spoke is a different criminal element, like drugs and weapons and cyber-terrorism and regular terrorism and all that other stuff you see on TV. There's even a spoke for people who sell kids. And the Ghost is at the center of the wheel. He's the guy who keeps the thing rolling. He connects everyone and helps them get what they need to commit their crimes. In turn, they pay for the privilege. And the Ghost is not above using people and throwing them away. Or worse. The last time our paths crossed, he tried to have us killed when we accidentally discovered he was Veronica Brooks's father. We came out on top that time, which definitely qualifies as amazing. But it's also a secret.

I smile blankly at Jane Ann. Toby jumps in, babbling about how he became obsessed over the summer with how our sense of smell can trigger happy emotions and invented this app to send smells via text, but before he can out himself and the Cookies app as not actually amazing, Charlotte interrupts.

"If I don't get some water," she says, fanning her face, "I might faint. For real."

"And believe me," I say quickly, "Charlotte is a fainter."

Jane Ann jumps to her feet. "We can't have that! To the dining hall!"

The dining hall is the Disney World of food. Floor-to-ceiling windows give the impression of being outside, although the air in here is cool and sweet. There are at least twenty-five stations visible from the entrance. Burgers, sushi, rice bowls, a noodle station, fresh-made sandwiches, five kinds of soups, desserts piled practically to the roof. The mac and cheese is dreamy. The salad bar is twelve miles long. There's a make-your-own-sundae station. They have *soda*. Sure, it's some natural organic blah-blah-blah soda, but still . . . *soda*. At Smith, we get demerits if we even mention the word.

Like a good tour guide, Jane Ann leads us right to the beverages. "After you've had your fill," she says, "might I suggest a quick visit to the lake? It's nice and cool out on the docks and really beautiful. Tranquil, even. I have to work on some Challenge preparations for tomorrow, but please just let me know if there is anything else you need." She extends yet another sincere welcome to Briar, shakes our hands, and finally takes her leave.

"Wow," says Charlotte as Jane Ann walks away.

"Yeah," Toby agrees.

"I don't think she meant 'wow' in the same way you do, Toby," I say. He blushes and buries his face in his soda. Toby is one of my best friends and he's a boy, so it's completely within the realm of possibility that other girls will like him and he will like other girls. But it still does something funny to my stomach every time I see evidence of it. It's a different feeling from the one I have when I'm around Owen Elliott, which is, I swear, no feeling *at all*.

"Any more school spirit and I might have barfed on my shoes," Charlotte comments.

"It was a lot," Izumi concurs.

"Was it real?" I ask.

"Teenagers are not known for that level of enthusiasm over, well, *anything*," Izumi points out. "I mean, we have our reputations to think about."

"I know," says Charlotte. "It was weird."

"You guys are just jealous," says Toby. He might be right. This cafeteria is to die for.

After we sample all the desserts and seven kinds of soda, we roll out the door, a little sick to our stomachs but satisfied. Charlotte and Izumi head back to the dorm while Toby goes off to check out the computer lab. I swipe a stack of chocolate chip cookies and follow signs to the docks. My footsteps are cushioned by a carpet of pine needles as I make my way through a large grove of trees. Birds chirp merrily overhead. Jane Ann is right. It's kind of tranquil down here.

A large wooden dock extends into the lake. Long narrow crew boats, or shells, are tied to cleats all along the edge, bobbing gently in the murky water. I kick off my shoes and take a seat, letting my feet dangle into the warm water. I wonder if I'd be a good rower or would I just fall in and that would be that? I think about this while I eat the stack of purloined cookies. I should have brought water. Now I'm thirsty.

I pull up my feet, drying them with my socks, when a blue-and-yellow butterfly lands on my remaining cookie. "Hello, friend," I say. "The cookies sure are good. Happy to share." The butterfly opens and closes its wings, its glittery stripes reflecting the sun. She's beautiful. As I bend down to take a closer look, the butterfly rises from the cookie and hovers at eye level. A mechanical whirring sound cuts through the sticky, still air. The butterfly flashes, like it just took my *photo*. On the horizon, a small dark cloud of blue and yellow closes in on my position.

"What the heck?" Suddenly, a few dozen butterflies buzz me, sticking in my hair, stinging my cheeks and neck, zooming at my eyes. I swat wildly with my hands.

"Go away! Stop it!" But this does little to deter them.

Eyes closed, I grab my shoes and run down the dock. Several butterflies follow, clinging to my hair. I stumble at the end of the dock, falling hard on my knees. It hurts, and there will be bruises, but I need to get out of here. I sprint across the green lawn between the sidewalks and dash through a lovely garden of late-blooming daylilies. The flowers leave trails of pollen on my legs. Charging into the dorm, I dash up the stairs and down the hall to our rooms. Izumi's door is slightly ajar, and I slam into it with my shoulder.

Izumi leaps from her bed, startled. "Abby, what the heck? Are you on fire?"

"Butterflies!" I holler, loud enough to bring Charlotte running. "Killer butterflies just attacked me down at the boat dock!"

Well, this gets their attention.

Chapter 7

THE COMPETITION.

AS WE STAND ON THE BOAT DOCK, Toby, Charlotte, and Izumi all agree the view is pretty good and that I'm insane. I didn't expect them to agree right away that I was attacked by a swarm of angry butterflies, but I hoped for at least a pause before they declared me off the rails.

"Butterflies don't sting," Izumi says. "They are not aggressive. And they don't buzz."

"They just hang around looking pretty," Charlotte adds.

"Maybe you just smell really good?" Toby offers. "Like a flower?"

"Jeez," I mutter. "Thanks."

"Whatever they were," Izumi says, "they're gone now. It's probably the heat."

"It was *not* the heat," I insist. "There was something weird about those butterflies. And there's something weird about this place."

"Because they have nice bathrooms?" asks Charlotte. "That feels judgy."

Right now, my instincts twitch. Not all is as it seems. But my instincts have been wrong before. And those butterflies left no evidence behind. Maybe I *do* smell like a flower?

"Everyone here is really nice," Toby says, in defense of Briar. "Especially Jane Ann. She gave me a tour of the computer facilities, and they are first-rate. She also said one of the teams participating in the Challenge built a nuclear weapon detection device that the government now uses."

"The bar is high," Izumi says.

They have moved on from my killer butterfly paranoia. They are probably right. I'm freaking out over nothing, just some impolite insects. Big deal. I should concentrate my freaking out on the Challenge competition, like everyone else. Still, I wish I'd caught one so I could figure out what was weird about them and prove to my friends that it wasn't the heat or my imagination.

At five o'clock, the Challenge teams gather in the

gaudy, enormous theater for the headmaster's welcome. The air-conditioning struggles in the heat. But it's the first time we get a good look at the competition. There are thirty teams of two, three, and four students. They come from all over the country. About one hundred of us pack into a single section of the theater, with the remaining seats filled by Briar students. The atmosphere is unhinged carnival. After all, the entire school gets the week off to spectate. There's a lot of cheering and yelling and high-fiving.

We sit directly behind Poppy and Owen Elliott. Owen Elliott offers a weak smile as greeting. It's possible Poppy has forbidden him from speaking to us. I pick out two Briar teams in our ranks. They chat amiably with the teams around them. Like Toby said, they are really *nice*. Jane Ann, our enthusiastic tour guide, sits a few rows away. Her hair is so shiny. How does she do that? She glances my direction and flat-out busts me for marveling at her hair. She offers a shy smile, and I return my gaze to the back of Owen Elliott's head.

On the ample stage, the Briar headmaster, a bald man in the same T-shirt and cargo pants as the students, calls for quiet. It takes a while. This is a rowdy crowd, willing to cheer just about anything.

"Welcome, visitors," Baldy begins, his amplified voice booming like thunder. He makes it sound like we are aliens in from outer space. "Are you as amazed by Briar as we are?" Cheers erupt. Baldy waggles his bushy eyebrows. "Two years ago, Briar was a nothing campus, a backwater, sad and irrelevant. But determination turned it around. Mark my words, we *will* be the premier boarding school in all the land!"

I glance at Charlotte, who grimaces. They are certainly piling it on. The team section responds with muted clapping because we don't really care about Briar being premier or platinum or whatever. Baldy's pate glistens with sweat. His face glows red. If he keeps this up, he might keel over. I bet that will get a lot of cheers too.

Onstage, Baldy shifts gears to the Challenge rules. No cheating. No bullying. No bribery. Bribery? The Challenge is meant to foster the spirit of camaraderie by means of healthy competition. Those of us sitting in the teams' section glare at one another, making it clear that camaraderie and health have no place in the Challenge. This is for blood. Win or die trying. The kids here are no joke.

"While you are with us on the beautiful Briar campus," Baldy drones, "we want you to feel at home. What is ours is yours. You may come and go as you please, use any of the facilities and enjoy your time here."

"They have a pastry chef on staff," Charlotte whispers. "Did you know that?"

"He makes croissants," adds Izumi. "Fresh. Everyday!"

My friends have fallen in love, and the object of their affection is Briar. Who knew they could be had for a decent croissant? Baldy invites us to join him for a special teams dinner at the main dining hall. He says it will be a good opportunity for us to get to know one another before the competition begins tomorrow.

"Good to know your enemy," Charlotte murmurs, squinting at the competition.

Baldy wraps it up with boring but important details—how to find the dining hall, how to get clean towels, how to access the Wi-Fi. I glance around. By this point, everyone is hot and dazed. Even the rowdy Briar students offer only limp cheers for the towels. Sweat runs from my scalp down my neck. My head itches. The idea that a swarm of butterflies could be attracted to my stink is really not that far-fetched. I scratch at my itchy head. There's something stuck in my hair. Great. Probably Poppy spat a wad of gum in there while I wasn't paying attention.

But it's no gum. A single glittery killer butterfly falls into my hand.

Chapter 8

DIRTY LAUNDRY.

THE DINING HALL REFLECTS THE PARTY MOOD.
Brightly colored banners embroidered with the names of all our schools hang from the ceiling. Dozens of rectangular tables cover the floor. Outside, torches flicker and reflect off the glass walls.

We sit at a table with Team OP and insult each other's chances of winning while collectively swooning over the food. Owen Elliott agrees to swim naked laps in the Cavanaugh Family Meditative Pond and Fountain if we even *place* in the Challenge. Poppy doesn't think naked swimming cuts it and wants a different, more humiliating task for us if we lose. This is getting ugly. Halfway through her sandwich, Poppy whips out a red leather notebook and starts writing frantically.

"What's that?" asks Charlotte.

"My idea book," Poppy says. "I just thought of something *brilliant*."

"What?"

"I can't tell you," she scoffs. "It's my intellectual property. It's valuable."

"Is she kidding?" Charlotte asks Owen Elliott.

"Not at all," Owen replies glumly.

"How many ideas do you get in a day?" I ask, unable to remember the last time I had even one good idea.

"Twelve today," she replies, "but sometimes as many as thirty or forty."

"I just lost my appetite," Charlotte says, shoving her plate away.

The butterfly is tucked safely in my pocket. I want to examine it up close before I show it to my friends. If it turns out to be a regular old butterfly, there is no need for me to suffer more humiliation for my freak-out.

We spend the rest of the evening in the palatial Briar games room. Pool, Ping-Pong, air hockey, classic video games like Pac-Man and Asteroids. Nothing violent but practically everything else. One wall contains shelves stacked high with board games and card games. My Smith comrades visibly drool, discussing the possibility of a midyear transfer. Even the Briar cheese fries, something Smith does well, are a step above. More humiliation.

Toby wants to have a confab about the competition tomorrow, but it's hard to concentrate when surrounded by all this *fun*. Finally, he threatens to quit, leaving us high and dry. This gets our attention. We follow him out of the game room.

"You guys are impossible," he says, exasperated.

"But I was about to get the high score on Pac-Man!" Izumi yells. "Sabotage!"

Toby forces us to sit down on some steps outside the building. I think they're marble steps, which is ridiculous, right?

"Tomorrow is a big deal," Toby begins. He's going to lecture us on being serious and doing our best. Sometimes he sounds like Drexel, even though I know better than to say that aloud. "We need to go in there and work hard. Statistically, whoever wins the first Challenge task, wins the entire competition. We can't mess up."

"Do we have any idea what the task will be?" asks Izumi. "I mean, I know it's secret, but can we guess?"

Toby grins. "I can do better than guess," he says. "An

analysis of past Challenges points toward clean water being a topic this year."

"Water?" I ask. That is not very exciting.

"I know what you're thinking, but almost a billion people on planet Earth don't have access to clean water," Toby replies. "And drinking contaminated water leads to all sorts of diseases and a lot of death. We will likely get a box full of junk, like duct tape and plastic piping and pieces of screen and things, with the task of inventing a water purification system that costs practically no money to make."

"This is scaring me," Charlotte says.

"Or," Toby says thoughtfully, "it might be toilets."

"Huh?"

"They might want us to build a toilet. 2.3 billion people in the world don't have access to a decent toilet. That means more contamination, more disease, and more death. Yeah. My bet is on water or toilets."

"Last Challenge theme was space travel," Izumi mutters. "They had to figure out a way to live on Mars."

"And we get toilets," Charlotte says flatly.

"It's more important than Mars," responds Toby. "It's also important to get enough sleep. We need to be our absolute best tomorrow. Now everyone go to bed."

We murmur agreement and say our good nights. And

when Toby disappears around a corner, we immediately dash back to the game room and stay there until campuswide lights out at ten o'clock. Finally, alone in my room, I pull out the butterfly and place it on the desk. It really does look like just a dead butterfly, even up close, and this is probably because it is. I poke it with a pencil. Nothing unusual. I need to get it together. I swipe it into my garbage can and go to bed.

At midnight, a persistent buzzing pulls me out of a bizarre dream about unicorns playing Fortnite. I rub my eyes and flick on the light. My phone, on the desk, is silent, and I didn't set the alarm on the clock beside the bed. What's making that noise? A dull blue light blinks on and off in the garbage can. I peer inside. My butterfly is buzzing and glowing, even though butterflies don't buzz and don't glow. And don't come back from the dead!

Gingerly, I scoop it out of the trash. Every time its body flashes blue, it emits a sharp buzzy tone. What does it mean? Is someone searching for it, or calling to it? Suddenly, having this drone butterfly in my room seems like a very bad idea. Holding it in the palm of my hand, I creep into the hallway. As I move toward the back of the building, the beeping quiets and flashing light weakens. Interesting. I swing around and head down the hall in the other direction. The light gets brighter and the beeping faster and louder. It must be homing in on its flight of butterfly friends. Or they are calling it home. Either way, I have to see what's on the other end, which means I have to get out of this building.

Like the Smith dorms, the doors here are locked and alarmed. Unlike Smith, the windows are alarmed as well. This is a problem. The window has always been my go-to escape route. Now what? I tiptoe down the hallway, assessing my options as the butterfly buzzes away in my closed fist. There aren't even any heating or air-conditioning ducts I can crawl through. The only way out is the laundry chute. At Smith, we are responsible for our own laundry. Each dorm has a collection of sad washers and dryers in the basement, and if a girl comes armed with four hundred quarters to feed the machines, she might eventually be rewarded with clean socks. Mostly, we just recycle stuff until it can walk to the laundry room of its own accord. But here at Briar, they have laundry *service*. Students bundle their dirty clothes in mesh bags labeled with their name and room number and toss them down a chute that leads, hopefully, to a way out of here.

I peer down the chute. It's really dark, and I will likely break a leg. And how do I explain *that*? I can't very well say

I accidentally fell down the laundry chute. Briar already has a poor opinion of every other school on the planet, and this will be confirmation that we are all idiots. Or maybe there is no way out of the laundry room and I have to wait for the service to show up tomorrow and collect the dirty clothes before I can get out. This will make me late for the nine-o'clock Challenge kickoff, which will lead to Toby killing me, which is worse than a broken leg. But I'm getting ahead of myself. *Just go down the chute and see what happens.*

It doesn't take long to figure out this is a bad idea.

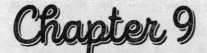

Chapter 9

CHUTES. NO LADDERS.

JENNIFER LOVES WATCHING *How the Grinch Stole Christmas.* She laughs so hard at Max the dog that sometimes I worry she will hurt herself. But the Grinch and his too-wide-for-the-chimney butt would empathize with how I'm stuck fast in the laundry chute. Or he'd mock me on account of his too-small heart. Either way, I can't move. Gravity has abandoned me.

The strong smell of lavender wafts up from below, and I gag. Twisting my torso, I push my shoulder into the sheet metal for leverage, which just makes everything worse. What next? How does a person shrink the width of her shoulders while wedged in a laundry chute? It's possible this question has never been asked in the history of the universe. I'm an original! And screaming for help will just get me busted. The butterfly glows dimly in my pocket.

In the end, it's wiggle for the win. Inch by agonizing inch, I squeeze down the chute. After many long minutes, there is light at the end of the tunnel. Literally. I must be near the bottom. My reaction is to breathe deep with relief, but that expands my upper body enough that I can't wiggle. *Take shallow breaths, Abby, or stay in here forever.*

When I finally tumble out into a cart of dirty clothes, sorted and ready for laundering, I'm both thrilled and grossed out. My face lands in a dirty pair of socks, and my legs tangle in muddy soccer shorts. I scramble free of the cart.

"That was too intense," I mutter, looking around. I pull out the killer butterfly. It's still intact but very quiet, meaning I must be farther away down here from the butterfly hub. Or the walls are too thick for the signal to penetrate. There are several industrial-size washing machines and dryers. A long table covered in neatly folded clothes stretches from wall to wall. It smells sweet, like fabric softener, and the air is charged with static electricity. There are no windows. It's like a cinder-block prison cell.

"At least our laundry room has *windows*," I say, even if

we don't have a planetarium and our headmaster is a luna-tic who makes us wear ties. The only door to the outside is alarmed, of course, and, after the chute, I have to work hard to convince myself to consider the ducts behind the dryer. My heart beats wildly at the idea.

The dryer is as tall as I am and weighs five times as much. Shoving it out of the way is not an option. When I'm in impossible situations, I often try to look at things from my friends' perspectives. What would Izumi do? Or Charlotte? Or Toby?

"Okay, calm down now, Abby," I say to the empty room. "Izumi would just muscle the thing aside. Charlotte would sweet-talk it, and Toby would take it apart and invent a dryer bot or something. Argh! This is not helping."

But maybe if I come down from the top? How about that? I flip over one of the carts to use as a step stool and climb up on the giant dryer. From here, I kick the silver duct hard enough to disconnect it from the machine, rais-ing a cloud of thick dust. It's like swallowing a mouth full of tiny bugs. I cough and hack dramatically, just to put off having to crawl in there. *Stop thumping, heart!*

It doesn't. I push myself off the top of the dryer and slip into the duct. It's about the same size as the chute, but because I'm horizontal, I make like Superman and push with my feet and pull with my hands. When movie characters crawl through heating ducts, they're usually burgling a giant diamond or something. And they make it seem glamorous when really it's just disgusting. Just when I'm about to give up hope, I spill face-first into the wet grass.

Freedom! The butterfly buzzes frantically in my pocket. I pull it out and, sticking to the shadows, set off in the direction of the planetarium. But the butterfly doesn't like that idea, so I turn toward the dining hall. Maybe it's hungry, because this gets it super excited. It buzzes and flashes all over the place.

I skirt around the building to the kitchen loading dock, where the food is delivered. The door is propped open with a plastic crate used to deliver gallons of milk. I slip inside. And suddenly, my butterfly goes bananas, pricking my palm with what feels like tiny little lasers.

"Ouch!" My hand flies open, and the butterfly zooms away. Oh, no! I dash after it through the gleaming industrial kitchen, complete with stainless steel walk-in refrigerators and massive prep tables. Pots large enough to swim in are stacked beside an eight-burner range. Three double-size ovens line a wall. My butterfly performs an acrobatic barrel roll and disappears around a corner. I'm about to rush after it when voices halt me in my tracks.

"Oh, look! Another one! Such busy butterflies." Laughter follows. I drop low and crawl around the corner to get a better view. It must be a pantry, a space twice the size of my dorm room stacked with staples like flour and sugar. Awkward towers of cans teeter precariously. Inside, two kids sit on large plastic containers labeled PEACHES and TOMATOES. Peaches holds what looks like an Xbox controller. My butterfly darts right for him, hovers, and then drops into his lap, still. He plucks it up, examines it, and finally tosses it into a bag that is filled with similar butterflies.

"Cool," says Tomatoes.

"Yeah," agrees Peaches. "I sent a bunch down to the lake today. Dive-bombed some kid. Hilarious!"

"Dude," chides Tomatoes. "That's, like, platinum-level stupid. You could have gotten caught."

"But it was *fun*."

Tomatoes shakes his head, as if Peaches is a total lost cause. Peaches grins like an idiot.

And suddenly, there is *Jane Ann* coming right toward me. I slither around the corner, out of sight as she strides purposefully into the pantry. *What is she doing here?*

"Did you retrieve all the butterflies?" she asks, without even saying hello. Wait a minute. Perky, rah-rah Briar Jane Ann has been replaced by terrifying cyborg Jane Ann.

Tomatoes and Peaches cower under Jane Ann 2.0's withering gaze. Tomatoes clutches his butterfly bag to his chest.

"Yes," he whispers. "I got them all back. I should be able to upload the test surveillance footage tomorrow."

"*Tomorrow?*" Jane Ann asks. This is clearly not the answer she wants.

"Tonight?" offers Tomatoes. Peaches quakes beside him, eyes downcast.

"You have one job," Jane Ann says, with a grimace. "That is to spy on our visitors." She leans in close to Tomatoes, who recoils, spilling his bag of drone butterflies all over the floor. Peaches's eyes are as wide as saucers. Mine are, too. They are using drone insects to help the Briar teams *cheat*?

I'm sorry, but that is taking the school-spirit thing just a little too far. Jane Ann loves Briar, but I had no idea the lengths to which she would go to make sure her teams win. "I need to know you and your stupid butterflies are capable if this is going to work. Get me the footage."

Tomatoes nods vigorously.

"And shut the door when you leave," she snaps. "You two are about as responsible as a bunch of cats." And that's the end of Jane Ann. Peaches drops to his knees, collecting drone butterflies while Tomatoes catches his breath.

"Dude," Tomatoes says. "Tell me again why we're doing this for her?"

"Dude," Peaches replies. "For the butterflies. We couldn't build them without her. No Jane Ann, no resources. And the butterflies are pretty cool, right? They actually *work*."

"They are pretty cool," Tomatoes says, visibly relaxing.

"I'm amazed by us."

"Me too."

"But we better get out of here and download that footage before Jane Ann has us exiled to Siberia, you know?"

Peaches scoops the last of their precious insects off the floor, and they are gone. But just as I'm about to follow them out of the kitchen, I notice a single butterfly, left behind. Maybe Toby can hack it and access the footage, see who they've been spying on. Scurrying into the pantry, I scoop it up, but when I hear footsteps in the hallway, I have no choice but to fling myself behind a tower of flour. Did they realize they are missing a butterfly?

No. They are back to shut the door.

Chapter 10

TRAPPED. WITH CUPCAKES.

OH, *NO*.

I leap to my feet and push on the heavy door, but it doesn't budge. I am locked in the pantry. On the bright side, at least I won't starve to death. I settle in against a bunch of rice sacks to think. But all I can think is I really need to get out of here and tell my friends about the cheating. And we have to bring this information to Baldy. He's not going to like it, but a cheating scandal involving his precious school would be worse. I pull on the door a few more times, but it's a lost cause. Toby will kill me if this makes me late for the first Challenge task. Seriously. This is a disaster. Why don't I take the time to plan things out?

Why do I just act on instinct? I'd kick myself if I knew how.

But rather than collapse in despair, I comb the pantry for something to take my mind off my woes. Two trays of pink cupcakes, complete with beautiful frosting flowers, fit the bill. By the time the first worker shows up at four o'clock in the morning to start breakfast prep, I've had one nap and six cupcakes.

Not exactly the best way to go into the first Challenge task. To make matters worse, I can't get back into the dorm until the doors unlock at six a.m. I spend two long hours on a bench regretting the cupcakes and many of the other decisions I've made in the last twenty-four hours. When I finally bump into Charlotte in the dorm hallway, I don't look lovely.

"What *happened* to you?" she asks. "And why do you smell so . . . floral, like fabric softener?"

"Don't ask," I mutter, nudging her aside and heading toward my room. I want a hot shower in my fancy bathroom. Otherwise, I might keel over. But Charlotte trails along behind me, sensing a story. I must look worse than I thought.

My smelly clothing in a heap, I stand under water as hot as I can bear. Charlotte sits on the closed toilet.

"Lavender," she says.

"Huh?"

"That's what I smell. Clouds of it. Start talking."

Even the shower is not a refuge. I pull open the door and stick my head out. "I went down the laundry chute."

"You did not." I slam the door shut in response. "You *did*! Why?"

"I needed to get out, and the windows are alarmed in this stupid place. Who alarms their windows? We're in the middle of nowhere!" I tell her about the butterfly in my hair and Peaches and Tomatoes and Jane Ann version 2.0 and the cheating. Something is rotten at Briar, despite its shiny veneer.

"Drone *butterflies*?" Charlotte asks. "For real?"

"A whole bag full. Hand me a towel." She tosses one over the top of the shower and I wrap myself up. I have to get rid of my clothes because even the whiff of lavender is making me gag. Lavender-aphobia. Is that a thing? I might have just invented it.

Izumi rolls into my room, yawning and stretching her arms, as Charlotte examines the butterfly. "What's that?" Izumi asks, collapsing on my bed.

"Oh, no big deal," Charlotte says casually. "Just a killer drone butterfly that Jane Ann is using to cheat in the Challenge."

This goes over exactly as expected. Izumi sits bolt upright. "What does *that* mean?"

I repeat the whole story, with Charlotte adding details for emphasis and drama. Izumi is impressed by my cupcake consumption. "Did you bring us any?"

"This is not about cupcakes," I snap.

"Touchy," says Izumi.

"Obviously, they plan to deploy their butterfly army this morning, when the Challenge task begins," Charlotte says. "Buzz into the rooms where teams are working and steal the best ideas."

"This is awful," Izumi says. "Gemma and Emma would be *so* disappointed."

"Good thing they're dead," Charlotte replies.

"Who do we report this to?" asks Izumi.

"Baldy," I say. "He's going to be sad."

"If he even believes you," Izumi says.

"You don't think he'll think I'm making it up, do you?"

Charlotte shrugs. "I kind of agree with Izumi. He's obsessed with being perfect. He's not going to like this development."

"So what do we do?"

"Evidence," Izumi replies. "We need that video footage to *prove* what Jane Ann is doing."

In short, we need Toby.

We find him at breakfast, fresh-faced and ready to crush the Challenge. "What's wrong with her?" he asks, pointing at me.

"I'm just hungry," I say quickly.

"She had a long night," adds Charlotte. She relays the details of my adventure to Toby as I stuff my face with fresh scrambled eggs and buttery croissants—real food to compensate for the cupcakes. Charlotte does a much better job with the story than I do. Toby is on the edge of his seat, mouth hanging open, coffee mug tilting precariously in his hand.

"Drone butterflies?" he whispers. "To *cheat*?" I pull the evidence out of my pocket and slide it across the table. Toby picks it up and gazes at it with awe.

"Brilliant," he whispers.

"Can you figure out where they are uploading the footage?" I ask. "So we can get it?" As the words tumble out, I spray my friends with bits of yellow egg.

Toby wipes it from his sleeve. "Gross."

"Sorry," I say. "The footage?"

"I can probably figure out where it's streaming to," he says.

But it's going to have to wait until later. The Challenge

is about to begin. Briar crackles with excitement. The day promises to be another hot one as hundreds of students move like a mob to the theater, with lots of laughing and screaming.

Back in the auditorium, I try not to stare at Jane Ann, but it's no longer about her hair. Baldy steps up to the microphone, sweating profusely. He removes his reading glasses and wipes them on his shirt. This just makes things worse. His lips squeeze into a tight little line. "Good morning, competitors," he says, tucking the useless glasses into one of his cargo pockets. "And welcome to the first day of the Challenge! Emma and Gemma Glass believed young people like yourselves could fix the world."

"I bet they never considered drone butterflies," Izumi whispers.

"And the world needs fixing," Baldy continues. "Now more than ever, your creativity and problem-solving skills are what it will take to right the wrongs, repair what is broken, and hand the next generation a better place to live." He pauses dramatically to let that sink in. The kid to my right yawns so widely I can see his dental work. *Come on, Baldy. Cut to the chase already. It's hot in here!*

"Water," Baldy says. Is he dehydrated? Is he going to faint? Should we call someone?

No. Turns out Toby is right, and water is this year's *theme*. Baldy holds up a clear plastic bottle half-full and shakes it. "Almost one billion people around the globe don't have access to this basic need that we take for granted. This year's Challenge tasks will focus on how we can get clean water to those billion people. You will need to be creative. You will need to think outside the box. Remember, the judges want to be *dazzled*. Now, for the task number one details. Please pay attention."

It's so quiet you could hear a pin drop. Everyone has collectively stopped breathing.

"Challenge task one is about creative engineering, about taking the ordinary and making it extraordinary." Toby and Izumi lean forward, eyes shining. They like the idea of creative engineering. "Each team will be given a cardboard box of items that can be found anywhere in the world. The boxes are the same and contain simple things, like duct tape and soda cans, screens and screwdrivers. Your task is to create something, a device or method, that can *clean* contaminated water."

I glance around at the surrounding teams, already plotting how to tunnel five miles into the earth and tap a geyser of pure fresh beautiful water, using nothing more than a pipe cleaner and a discarded T-shirt.

"A water purifier," Toby whispers reverently.

"Yeah," Izumi says with a sigh.

Charlotte stares at them. "You guys are made for this," she says.

Here's how it works. Teams are assigned to different buildings on campus and given that cardboard box of junk. Twenty-four hours later, bring the dazzle or get killed on points. The Challenge judges don't care if you eat or sleep during that twenty-four hours. They don't care if you dance a jig or brush your teeth. Dazzle is the name of the game.

Chapter 11

SMARTS.

BALDY READS OUT BUILDING ASSIGNMENTS.
We're in the engineering library, along with two other teams, and Team OP is in the main library. Entering the engineering library, we trade false smiles and insincere "good lucks" with the other teams and peel away to our assigned room on the third floor. Inside is a large box atop a long table, surrounded by a few chairs. Sun beats through the large uncovered windows.

"Ready?" Toby asks, clutching the box. We nod. He dumps the supplies onto the table. There is duct tape, wire, several pairs of pliers, squares of screen, tiny bits of unidentifiable metal, hunks of hard clear plastic in different shapes, cotton balls, Q-tips, and more. But where I see a pile of junk, my friends see possibilities.

"I have a great idea!" Izumi cries.

"Me too!" Toby yells.

"So many possibilities!" Izumi shifts through the materials. "If we take the screen and the soda can . . . ," she begins.

"And we use the cotton . . . ," Toby adds.

"With the metal spring . . ."

"Brilliant! Yes! And then the pliers . . ."

"Why didn't I think of that? Of course. With the plastic!" Izumi glances at us as if just realizing we're in the room. "What do you guys think?"

Charlotte's eyebrows zoom up to her hairline. "I think we think whatever you think," she says. I nod vigorously in agreement.

While Toby and Izumi argue their way toward a prototype design that is likely to save the most lives in the real world and therefore bring the dazzle, Charlotte watches them like a spectator at a tennis match.

At midnight, all the teams continue to work with feverish determination. I keep a vigil for evil butterflies, but none appear. Our work space is littered with empty soda cans and candy wrappers. A cafeteria tray laden with dirty dishes sits in a corner. Toby's eyes pinwheel in his head. He scoffs at the suggestion of a nap.

"I'll sleep when I'm dead," he says. And I know better than to urge him to take a break and bring me some butterfly evidence. I hate the fact that Jane Ann is going to swing this contest in favor of her beloved Briar before anyone can stop her, but getting in Toby's way right now is a bad idea.

While Toby and Izumi do most of the serious project work, they delegate the boring tasks to us. Right now, I'm soldering two coils of wire together into a precise U shape. I have no idea what for, and when I ask, they yell at me to get back to work.

When it becomes clear we are staying up all night, Charlotte and I decamp to the dining hall, open twenty-four seven during the Challenge, to get strawberry cheesecake, because everyone knows an all-nighter *needs* cheesecake. Izumi and Toby don't even look up. Outside, the night has turned sultry, the air thick with humidity. Lights glow in the buildings where teams work diligently on their projects. It's quiet outside. Every kid who is not participating in the Challenge is long asleep. The path to the dining hall is all but deserted, which is why we notice Jane Ann in the first place.

Head down, she walks quickly, throwing furtive glances over her shoulder. Charlotte nudges me. "Hey. Look who it is. Cyborg girl. Maybe she is up to more no good?" We pause in a shadow, unseen, and watch her for a moment.

"Are you thinking what I'm thinking?" I whisper.

"Probably," responds Charlotte. The cheesecake all but forgotten, we wait about thirty seconds before setting off after Jane Ann. Who knows when Toby gets to the butterfly, but maybe Jane Ann leads us to different evidence of her cheating ways right *now*. She loops around the engineering library, past the arts building, and right up to the door of one of the boys' dormitories.

"Should we feel bad we left Toby and Izumi?" I ask.

"Honestly, I'm not sure they even knew we were there." That sounds reasonable. We creep forward for a better view as Jane Ann marches up to the building door and strides right in as if she belongs. Which she doesn't. *No girls in the boys' dorm and no boys in the girls' dorm* is a boarding school gold standard rule, but it apparently doesn't apply to Jane Ann. And her key card. Glancing at each other, we run right after her.

"And I was worried the Challenge wouldn't be fun," Charlotte whispers as we slip through the door, just before it closes, and in time to see Jane Ann disappear around a corner. We follow, creeping through the dark empty hallway like burglars, clinging to the shadows. When she knocks on the door for room twenty-seven, a disheveled Tomatoes answers the door. His eyes fly open in alarm.

"What time is it?" he asks.

"Time for you to stop being a screwup," Jane Ann hisses, waving a flash drive in his face.

"But the footage is great," Tomatoes protests. "The butterflies did their job."

"I *specifically* asked for the Smith School team," she says. "So *where* is the footage?" At the mention of Smith, Charlotte squeezes my thigh so hard, I almost scream. What's so *special* about Team OP anyway?

"It's in there," Tomatoes replies meekly.

"There are two minutes of them discussing the dining hall *milkshakes*!" Jane Ann is about to blow. She's about to wake up about one hundred sleeping boys, but she doesn't care.

"The milkshakes are really good," whispers Tomatoes. *Oh, Tomatoes, that was the wrong answer!*

"Do you want to *keep* your butterflies?" Jane Ann hisses. "Do you want me to turn you in for *cheating*?"

"You *wouldn't*."

"You don't think?"

Tomatoes recoils. "I'm . . . I'm sorry . . . I can redeploy

the butterflies . . . get the info on Smith that you want. I swear."

"Last chance," Jane Ann says, grimly. "Do it now. Don't fail me again." She leaves a breathless Tomatoes behind.

"Boy, she is taking this school spirit thing *way* too far," he mutters, collecting himself. Charlotte elbows me in the ribs.

"Just how far is she willing to go in the name of Briar?" she whispers. If I had to guess, I'd say all the way.

Back in the engineering library, Izumi asks us if we went somewhere. They didn't even notice we were gone! Toby says they are in the zone and have to take advantage of it while it lasts.

"It's like we are laser focused," he says. The project, a cheap and accessible way to filter water, comes together on the table. It looks like the cardboard box barfed out its contents and Toby and Izumi wrapped it all up in duct tape. But I know better than to say this aloud.

"We, ah, discovered something," I say casually, circling the table.

"Jane Ann is out for Team OP," Charlotte says. Without pause, she launches into the details of our infiltration of the boys' dormitory. Izumi and Toby fall out of the zone with a thud.

"I guess she thinks they are the ones to beat," Izumi offers.

"I'm insulted," Toby says.

"We'll tell Baldy first thing in the morning," I say. "Even without evidence." My team nods in agreement. But for now, it's back to work.

Time to bring the dazzle.

Chapter 12

WINNING ISN'T EVERYTHING.

THE CHALLENGE JUDGING IS HELD in a sweeping multipurpose room. The air is pungent with the stink of unbrushed teeth. Contagious yawns tear through the crowd like the Great Plague of London. At assigned tables, teams unpack cardboard boxes and set up projects. None of them are going to win any awards for beauty, including ours. But beauty is not the point. Function is.

I do a lap around the room, trying to find Baldy, but he is nowhere to be found, which is strange considering the Challenge seems to be the highlight of his life. The few people I ask shrug their shoulders. No idea. But it will have to wait. The judges have entered the great room.

They systematically move around, sidestepping spectators and evaluating each effort. Right away, I notice Jane Ann parked next to Team OP. Did she get the footage she wanted last night of Team OP's design and is here to gloat? I have no great love for Team OP, but I hate the idea that Jane Ann's cheating more. Gemma and Emma would be so disappointed! I stride over to their table.

"Good morning, fellow Smith team!" I bellow.

Poppy crosses her arms defensively. "What do you want?"

"Just saying hello."

"Fine. You said it. Now leave."

Nice. If only she knew what I know . . . but she can't know, because who knows what would happen if I told her? I turn my attention to Owen Elliott, hoping to distract him with my dazzling smile.

"Did you guys stay up all night?" I ask. "What did you build?"

Poppy literally puts her body between Owen Elliott and me. The edge of her red idea notebook peeks out of her pocket. "Tell her nothing. She's the enemy."

Jane Ann watches this scene unfold with a clinical gaze.

"Oh, come on," I say. "We're both playing for the same school."

"You know how I feel about that," growls Poppy.

"But what about the rest of your team?" I try to peer around her to make eye contact with Owen Elliott, but Poppy plays good defense. This pleasant back-and-forth is interrupted by Jane Ann. She gets down at eye level with Team OP's water-cleaning device.

"Wow," she says. "This is . . . amazing. So intricate and smart."

Poppy blushes. "Just a little something I whipped up."

"We," Owen Elliott interrupts. "Something *we* whipped up."

"Oh, yeah," says Poppy, eyes never leaving Jane Ann. "Him, too, I guess."

Is Jane Ann building her up so when Briar wins it stings more? This feels low even for Jane Ann.

"I was just telling my friends about how you guys are really the next level up," Jane Ann says. "We admire you *so* much."

I roll my eyes. "Really?"

"Abby, shut up and go away." Poppy returns her attention to her adoring subject. "I pride myself on being an inventor." And off she goes, explaining the agonizing details of Blackout to a riveted Jane Ann. A good spy can tell when something is off—they can feel it in the air or in their gut—but Poppy has no idea that Jane Ann has less than the best intentions.

I gesture for Owen Elliott to come with me. He looks relieved as he slowly backs away from the inaugural meeting of the Poppy Fan Club to a discreet distance. "Don't ask me anything that can compromise me with Poppy, okay?" he says quickly. "I *need* this Challenge win. You don't understand."

"I don't?"

He sighs and, for a flash, looks ten years older, and tired. "My parents. Bragging rights. Like, *Owen Elliott won another prestigious award, so this week we like him.*"

I feel a twinge of sadness. Winning would be nice, of course, but I can't imagine Jennifer liking me *more* because of it. Don't his parents know that when Tucker Harrington III shoved Miles Broadus into the Cavanaugh fountain, Owen Elliott jumped right in there and fished him out? And that fountain is disgusting. There are fish. And algae. Plus, he tolerates Poppy! He might even have found something legitimate to like about her. His parents have no right being mean to him. I feel a hot wave of hostility toward two people I've never met.

"Can you, I don't know, tell them it bugs you?" I ask.

He snorts. "Are you kidding? It would just give them another thing to fight about."

"I'm sorry," I offer.

He stares at the space above my head. "It's okay," he mumbles. "It is what it is."

"Hey, did you happen to notice any butterflies in your work space last night?" I ask casually.

"Butterflies? Like, in the room?"

Oh, man. I sound like a lunatic. There's an awkward pause. Come to think of it, most of my interactions with Owen Elliott are awkward. It's possible I'm blushing.

"Never mind," I say. "I hear you are the reigning world champion at Asteroids. I totally stink, and I don't know how much longer I can take Toby mocking me over it. Want to meet up at the game room later and you can give me some tips?"

His face lights up, and my stomach does a weird twisty thing that is surprising but not entirely unwelcome. "Yeah," he says. "Cool."

Our moment is interrupted by Charlotte howling for me to get back to the table. The three men and three women judges wear khaki pants, blue blazers, and stern expressions. The tall woman clicks her pen open and closed, open and closed. This is no laughing matter. The judges examine our work without smiling. They pour brownish water through the filter and dip bits of paper in the water that comes out the other side to test it for quality. They mutter and mumble and record numbers on their clipboards. I am absolutely sure they are part of the cyborg army. After a few minutes, they move on to the next table and repeat the whole ghastly process.

In the end, we take fifth. First place goes to Team OP. One of the Briar teams pulls second. Poppy preens her glorious feathers, accepting congratulations like a member of the royal family. Toby clenches his fists.

"I have never come in fifth in anything ever before," he growls. He glares at the celebrating Smith team. I'm worried he might go over there and do something foolish. In my experience, food is a fail-safe distraction when it comes to Toby,

"Lunch!" I shout. "Wouldn't that be good right about now?" I link an arm through Toby's and haul him away. "And don't worry. We will win the next round."

"I'm going to hack that butterfly," he says, eyes steely. "Right now. *Fifth* place. Jeez."

Nothing motivates like losing.

Chapter 13

THE ADULTS ARE UP TO NO GOOD.

WE ARE MEANT TO TAKE THE AFTERNOON off and relax before the Challenge continues tomorrow. Of course, even though we are all zombies desperately in need of sleep, everyone heads immediately for the game room. Toby is so distracted by losing, he even agrees to let me play Monster Madness 3.0 on his lightning-fast gold phone while he hacks the butterfly and I set off in search of Baldy, who never showed up this morning. And my face is buried in the game, which is why I don't see the very man I'm looking for until we crash into each other full force. My chocolate chip cookie stash goes flying. I just barely hold on to the phone.

"Watch where you're going," Baldy says sharply as I sprawl to the floor. "I'm in an incredible rush." His phone is pressed to his flaming red ear, and sweat drips from his eyebrows onto the folder he carries. Without an apology or offer of assistance, he steps over me, squashing a perfectly good chocolate chip cookie, and charges on his way.

Jennifer says that people tell you everything you need to know without saying a word, and right now Baldy is telling me something is not right. Sure, it might be a student who fell in the lake and got bit by a trout, but it might be something else. But between the look on his face and his no-show this morning, I'm betting it's not fish-related. Before I'm even conscious of my decision, I've abandoned the cookie mess and am hot on Baldy's heels as he practically runs for the exit.

I stay hidden behind the open doors as outside on the massive steps, he collides with Jane Ann. He does not look happy to see her. He looks like his head might explode. Was she waiting for him? Is this a *meeting*? My pulse quickens.

"You promised me you'd get it done," he barks. "Everything depends on it!" Jane Ann regards him with disgust.

"You need to calm down," she replies, cool as a cucumber. "I *am* getting it done. In the time frame you asked for. Don't blame me for your mistakes."

Baldy runs his hands over his head as if he actually has hair there. He shakes the folder at her, and several papers escape, dancing in the wind at his feet. He barely notices. "Just get it done," he hisses. "I'll talk our way into more time."

As Baldy drops down to his knees to begin collecting the contents of the folder, Jane Ann gives him a look full of pity. "You'd better," she says.

I wedge myself behind the door as she glides by. If I had to guess, I'd say she's off to commit more crimes against Gemma and Emma Glass, but what do I know? Outside in the elegant school driveway, lined with shrubs cut to look like Greek gods, a black car pulls up. The driver pops the trunk and opens the rear passenger door. Where is Baldy going? *Who* is he going to beg for more time and *why*? When the driver notices Baldy crawling around on the ground collecting papers, he leaps to his assistance, and I leap in the open trunk, pulling it swiftly closed. My heart races. It's a large trunk, all things considered, and not too uncomfortable. Really, I'm pretty lucky. It could have been a Smart Car chauffeuring Baldy. That would have required the human pretzel approach.

Of course, the bumpy pavement doesn't feel so good. The gold phone, which I *still* have, which means Toby is going to kill me, indicates we've been driving for fifteen minutes toward Hartford. I silence the phone to avoid detection and follow along on the GPS as we wind along the tangle of roads outside the city. Traffic is bad. I spend the time crunched up, getting to know the new spy phone.

I scroll through the pages of apps, some familiar and some I don't recognize. Judging by their names, it's probably not a good idea to test them in a confined space. Like a blaring horn? That can't end well. There's also a lightning bolt, a swarm of bees (more insects—great), a snarling dog, and a tray of fresh-baked cookies. This must be the app that Toby practically poisoned himself with. I keep my thumb far from that one. It would be extra bad in the trunk of a car.

Right around when my legs start to cramp, the car glides to a stop. The GPS indicates we're at the Wadsworth Atheneum, which I happen to know is the oldest public art museum in the country. And I know this because I spent an afternoon here with Jennifer. She told me it was because they have an outstanding collection of American Impressionist paintings and Hudson River School landscapes, but really it was to meet a contact.

The car grinds to a halt. Doors open and slam. Baldy's muffled voice comes through the seams of the trunk. I can't very well jump out and follow him, but it seems a safe bet he's going into the museum. The car moves again, a little farther down the street and into a parking garage. I wait five minutes before popping the trunk with the glow-in-the-dark emergency handle. The driver covers his face with a Red Sox cap and snores softly. It takes a full minute of dancing from one foot to the other to get the blood back into my extremities. Lucky for me we didn't drive to Miami.

I head out to the sidewalk and jog toward the museum. Thankfully, kids get in free, because I'm not exactly prepared for a museum outing. A nice lady in a blue cardigan comments on how wonderful it is for me to be visiting the museum. She does not seem fazed that I am alone and not in school. She tells me not to miss the special exhibit with Rembrandt's drawings.

"Oh, they are divine," she says with a sigh.

"Have you seen a bald man?" I ask casually. "Sweaty, in a rush?"

"The anxious one?" she says, without missing a beat. "Certainly. About ten minutes ago."

"My father," I say, with an exaggerated eye roll.

"He asked for directions to the American Decorative Arts gallery," she offers.

"He has a thing for fancy furniture," I say, with a shrug meant to convey general exasperation with parental units. I don't think she gets it, but she points me in the right direction and I take off at a fast clip but not so fast as to be suspicious. Not that there is anyone here to wonder.

Chapter 14

WELL, THIS IS . . . UNEXPECTED.

BALDY IS INDEED in the large Decorative Arts gallery. He stares at a silver tankard mug made by Paul Revere Jr. Junior did not ride through the night in April 1775 yelling, "The British are coming! The British are coming!" but he was a mean silversmith. I hunker down next to a tall display case holding an old Eli Whitney pistol.

Soon, another man shows up. He wears a gray suit with a colorful scarf rather than a tie. When he taps Baldy on the back, the Briar headmaster practically jumps out of his skin. These are not old friends. The two men sit down on a bench about ten feet from where I huddle. They whisper, but I can still hear them.

"Did you bring the information?" Scarf asks, eyes dark.

"I'm close," Baldy says. Sweat pours off his brow despite the air-conditioning.

"Close?" Scarf asks. *"Close?"*

"I'll have it in the next few days," Baldy says quickly. "I promise. I swear."

"In return for the information, you get a decade of Briar dominance of the Challenge. But my boss is not a patient man. Did he mention what happens if you fail?" Scarf drags his finger across his neck in a slicing motion, and Baldy goes pale. His Adam's apple bobs up and down as he swallows repeatedly.

"I'll get it. I'll get it," Baldy blubbers. "The Smith team is clueless. I just need an opportunity to steal what we need. Tell your boss it's coming."

Wait a minute! Baldy is trading Team OP secrets to this guy for guaranteed Challenge wins? And Jane Ann is in charge of securing the secrets? And I thought Gemma and Emma would be upset about the butterflies! This takes cheating to a whole new level. What on earth does Poppy have in that perky little head of hers that gets Baldy ten years of Challenge victories?

Scarf considers Baldy's words. "My boss would say that

opportunities don't appear. They are made. When he runs out of patience, you will know."

"It's under control," Baldy whispers. Scarf extends his arm to shake hands, and when he does, his sleeve rides up, revealing the fleshy inside of his wrist.

And there, for all the world to see, is a *triangle tattoo*. Not just any triangle. A very specific triangle, each segment thick and colorful.

I might throw up. The room suddenly swims before me. How can this *be*?

"Excuse me?" I look up to find a uniformed security guard standing over me, concerned. "What seems to be the problem?"

Uh-oh. I pitch quickly forward to my hands and knees. "Contact lens," I say, pointing at my eyeball and squinting. "On the floor here somewhere." The guard joins my search with murmurs of sympathy. "Or it might have fallen out over there." On all fours, I crawl out of the gallery. The guard crawls out too. Talk about doing whatever you can for your patrons. We stay low until it's safe to stand, at which point I pronounce the search a lost cause, thank the man for his help, and dash for the exit.

I'm panting hard by the time I reach the parking garage,

just in time to see Baldy climb into the back of the car and drive away, leaving me stranded in Hartford. Not that I could have flagged him down and asked for a ride exactly. I pull up Izumi's number on the spy phone. She seems the one least likely to yell at me.

"Is that you, Abby?"

"Yeah."

"I found her!" Izumi bellows, presumably to Toby and Charlotte. Toby immediately starts howling in the background. I try not to listen to the actual words because they are not very nice, but the gist of it is I should not have taken his fancy phone on a joyride without permission. And I should never have silenced it. Charlotte wrestles it from Izumi.

"Why are you in Hartford?" she asks.

It's comforting to know they care enough to track me. "I followed Baldy. He's in on it with Jane Ann. But that's not the worst of it. I have *bad* news." She puts me on speaker, and I relay the details from the Wadsworth Athenaeum. When I get to the part about the triangle tattoo, there is silence. My hands shake.

"Do you think it's, you know, the *Ghost*?" Izumi whispers.

"Maybe the guy is just in the isosceles fan club?" Toby offers. "Loves triangles?"

"Baldy is trading information about Team OP to the Ghost to guarantee Briar wins the next five Challenges," Charlotte says. "Is that right?"

"Pretty much," I reply.

"But whatever the Ghost wants, Baldy hasn't gotten it yet."

"Exactly."

"And here I was thinking we were done with the Ghost," Izumi muses, calmer than she has any right to be.

"That would be nice," adds Toby, "but this just got much bigger than Briar cheating on the Challenge. What does Team OP have that is so *valuable* to the Ghost?"

"I don't know," I say. "But we better figure it out."

"We should call Jennifer," Izumi says.

Izumi is right. This is the Ghost we're talking about here, and he's no laughing matter. "We'll call when I get back."

"I'm sending a car for you," says Charlotte, "even though Toby says I should just leave you there, but I kind of miss you."

"Gee, thanks." She makes some kissy noises on her end and hangs up.

It's blazing hot, so I stand up against the museum in a patch of shade, tucking the phone into the waistband of my shorts. A woman strolls down the sidewalk, dressed head to toe in black with spiky high heels and a fedora just so on her bleached-blond head. She has red lipstick and dark sunglasses that cover half her face. How can she stand it? I sweat just looking at her. She slows as she approaches, and if I were smarter and better and more *exceptional* I'd know something is up. But I'm not.

And that's how she grabs me and shoves me into a waiting SUV, just like that.

I don't even have time to protest before I'm blindfolded with my hands cuffed behind my back. I'm just assuming this is not the ride Charlotte ordered for me and I'm being kidnapped.

"We meet again," says the lady in black. *Oh, that voice!*

Fortunately, I'm not gagged. "Tinker Bell?" I yell. "Are you kidding me?"

Can this day get *any* worse?

Chapter 15

TINKER BELL FLIES AGAIN.

MY LAST ENCOUNTER WITH TINKER BELL was just outside of San Francisco, after being snatched by one of her kite-surfing henchmen and whisked across the bay at speeds that made me very nervous. We didn't have the pleasure of meeting face-to-face that time because I escaped, but her high-pitched, squeaky, whiny cartoon voice is unmistakable.

"Is that what you call me?" she asks, gleeful. "Tinker Bell? Oh, I *love* her! Sassy little thing giving Peter Pan fits."

I wiggle around in the seat, trying to find a comfortable position with my hands bound behind my back. *No way.*

Impossible. I hitch forward so my face is near my knees, and this offers some relief but lacks dignity.

"What do you want?" I grumble. Tinker Bell is the Ghost's competitor. She has been trying to out-bad him for years and apparently is doing a commendable job. Her network of evil doesn't quite match the Ghost's, but she sure is trying. In San Francisco, she wanted to use me for the same reason the Center did: to lure out my mother and finally be able to put a face to her rival. Knowledge is power, even if it is for unsavory purposes.

"I want to know what you're doing here," Tinker Bell says.

"I'm here because you dragged me off the sidewalk," I snap.

"Everyone is so touchy in this heat. You know what I mean. Confess."

"Or what?"

"You won't like it if I tell you."

"Really?"

"Somehow I knew you'd be difficult," she says. "Okay, I'll go first. A few months ago, the Briar headmaster reached out to my people. He wanted to guarantee his teams would win this competition everyone is so irrationally worked up over. I told him I only deal with professionals and he should crawl back under his rock. But then I got curious. And I had him tailed. Turns out my favorite competitor took him up on his offer. You know who I'm talking about, right? Well, that made me so curious I thought my head might explode. Because I really want to *find* him. Just so we can chat. Anyway, we're following the headmaster and then, boom, there *you* are. I don't believe in coincidences. Talk."

"How about you take off my handcuffs first?" I ask.

Tinker Bell snorts. "Nice try, kid. No way."

But she does rip off my blindfold. Up close, she's about Jennifer's age, with a thick layer of pancake makeup settling into the fine lines around her mouth and along her forehead. Her lipstick bleeds a little around the edges. She doesn't remove her sunglasses, so I can't see what she's thinking.

The gold smartphone is tucked in the waistband of my shorts. My hands are tied, but Toby's devices always include voice activation. With my original spy phone, I had to yell, *Toby is cool!* to get it to work. But I have no idea what the words are for this one. And the spy phone doesn't help me if I can't use it. I need a plan. I can jump out of the moving car. Not a great idea. I can scream. Pointless. I can beg. Yeah, right. Clearly, I need to kill time while I come up with a better plan.

"Okay," I say finally. "Baldy went to the museum to meet some guy. He was supposed to hand over information, but he didn't have it. Threats were made."

"Baldy?" Tinker asks, confused.

"The headmaster," I reply.

"Do you have nicknames for *everyone*?"

"How else am I supposed to keep them straight in my head?" I ask.

"Maybe use their real names?" Tinker suggests.

"Why would I do that?"

Tinker removes her glasses and rubs the bridge of her nose. "Kids. Honestly." She puts the glasses back on with an exaggerated sigh. "How do you know what Baldy and the man in the suit talked about?"

"I spied on them." *Duh.*

"Details."

I find it curious she does not ask me why I was following Baldy. She's not interested in backstory or motivation. She just wants the dirt.

"That's all I've got," I say. We've left the urban landscape behind and drive through a lush tunnel of trees at a speed that might result in us getting arrested. Which would be a good thing, but I can't rely on it.

"Who was the man?" Tinker asks.

I shrug. "Don't know."

"Nickname?"

"Scarf."

"Why am I not surprised?"

"I like to be consistent."

"You're not very helpful."

"That's what my mom says." Jennifer also says that if a person relies on GPS all the time, the part of her brain needed for navigation won't develop. So guess what? I have a great sense of direction. And we are not headed for Briar Academy. We're headed west.

I have to get out of this car.

Chapter 16

ACT CASUAL. DON'T PANIC.

JENNIFER ALSO SAYS scared people make stupid mistakes. Therefore, stay calm even if all signs indicate panicking would be appropriate.

"Where are we going?" I ask, trying to sound unconcerned.

"Just a little ride," Tinker Bell says. "I want to make sure you're being straight with me, telling me everything you know."

"I am!" Except for the parts I'm not.

"We'll see soon enough." Yeah. I really have to get out of this car. Jumping is back on the table as an option. Twisting my torso so my hands are wedged against the car door, I try the handle. It's locked, and there is no mechanism to unlock it. *Why* do the bad guys always have escape-proof cars?

Desperate, I decide on the snarling dog app. It seems the least likely to kill me as a snarling dog can't really materialize from a phone, can it? Boy, I hope not. Now to figure out how to make it work. Start with the basics.

"Dog!" I yell.

Tinker Bell must have dozed off, because she starts awake and glares at me over the tops of her sunglasses. Her hazel eyes are sharp and outlined with black liner. "Excuse me?"

"Nothing," I say. "I burped. Excuse me."

She glares at me for a moment before settling back in to nap. I let a few more minutes pass until her jaw goes slack with sleep. Maybe Toby reused his original password. I could see him thinking that's hilarious. Only one way to find out. "Toby is cool!" I shout.

Nothing! But Tinker jolts awake and grabs my thigh, digging in with the red talons. "Stop. Doing. That," she hisses.

"Yes, ma'am," I say, knowing full well I can't stop. Every minute I wait, I'm closer to whatever torture they have planned for me. I watch some more scenery go by.

The trees wilt in the heat, drooping toward the earth as if broken-hearted. Oh, wait a minute. Broken hearts. Toby pines for Veronica, still nursing his unrequited crush. It's worth a try.

"Veronica!" I yell. "Dog!" The phone erupts in furious growling, barking, and snarling. It's so realistic the driver immediately panics. The phone grows hot against my skin, but without my hands there is nothing I can do but take it. Tinker Bell is fully awake, screaming, but I can't hear her above the din. The driver, trying to cover his ears and drive with his knees, swerves perilously close to the heartbroken trees. Before Tinker can get her claws on me, I scramble from the backseat and tumble into place beside the driver.

"Hey!" He swings at me with one hand. I lean out of the way. The dog noise continues to emanate from the phone. It's chaos inside the SUV. From behind, Tinker Bell grabs my hair. I twist and turn to get away, my scalp howling in protest. My fingers are on the door handle. I pull it several times to release the lock, and it springs open, so I half hang out of the moving car. The driver gets ahold of my foot. I kick hard, but he tightens his grip. It's too bad. I really like these shoes. I curl my toes, and the sneaker flies off. I tumble backward out the open door.

Veronica speaks to me in my head. *Tuck and roll! Protect*

your brain! Protect your neck! In the split second before I hit the pavement, I curl into a tight ball, landing with a *thud* on the soft dirt shoulder.

The dirt is better than pavement, but it still hurts. A lot. Up ahead, the SUV tilts on two wheels, banking a U-turn. They are not giving up. I still can't get to the phone with my hands cuffed behind me, and it takes yelling, "Veronica! Off!" three times before it stops growling. I need to disappear in these woods, and traveling with a pack of angry dogs will not help.

Charging headlong into the trees, I squeak with pain every other step as the sticks and rocks poke through my sock into my foot. Sweat pours down my face. Leaves on the forest floor swirl as I run, my balance thrown off by my bound arms. In the distance, a door slams, and I hear Tinker Bell yelling at the driver to hurry up and find me.

I stumble down a small incline and land on my knees in a stream. It's unlikely the driver guy has finely honed tracking skills, but I decide to hedge my bets and stay in the water. The rocks are slippery, and I take at least one header before a hairpin turn puts me out of sight. I climb out and tuck in behind a clump of young trees. Driver guy isn't visible, but I hear him stumbling around in the woods, cursing my existence. And Tinker Bell's, too.

After a while, he quits. The SUV starts up with a roar, and with squealing tires, they take off. I crawl out of my hiding place, soaked and muddy with twigs in my hair and burrs stuck to my socks. Veronica is back in my head as I try one of her tricks to get free of the handcuffs. Tucking my legs to my chest, I maneuver my arms under my feet. If I were a rubber band, this would be easy. However, I'm a girl. "Uncomfortable" is not the word for it.

"Stop complaining," says Veronica, in my head. "You can't go through life with your hands tied behind your back."

"I *know* that," I say, grunting with the effort.

"Get it done," she says. "You can whine later."

"I'm not whining," I growl. "I'm screaming in agony. There is a difference."

Thankfully, she has nothing to say about that. My shoulders ache and throb. With a final push, I loop my body through my arms, and just like that, my hands are in front of me. I examine the zip-tie cuffs, made from thick hard plastic. At least they aren't metal.

A sharp rock in the stream will do the trick. I set to scraping the cuffs along the rock's edge, back and forth, fast and hard, until the smell of burning plastic fills the air.

It takes forever. Gnats swirl around my sweaty head.

Mosquitoes buzz my ears. Finally, with a quick *snap*, I yank the cuffs apart, leaving me with two unfashionable plastic bracelets. I can live with that.

I take stock. I'm down a shoe, my wrists are red and raw, and it's going to take a month of grooming to get the debris out of my hair. Toby's gold spy phone has left a nasty red rectangle on my skin, and, to make matters worse, the screen is cracked.

"Great!" I yell into the empty woods. "Just great."

I tap the fractured face a few times, but the battery is dead. Trudging through the underbrush, I eventually hit the road and head back in the direction from which we came.

Walking along the shoulder, I count the passing cars. Zero. My lone shoe leaks water. Every twenty steps, I check the phone again to see if it somehow has magically recharged. It hasn't. Finally, a dented red Honda happens around the bend, fishtailing to a dusty halt before me. An arm extends out the window and waves me on.

"Hurry up!"

This is the moment I have to decide whether to flee back into the words or creep close enough to see who is in the driver's seat. My feet hurt, so I take a chance on this being a simple act of kindness and not another abduction.

Behind the wheel is a young woman, probably Veronica's age. Her brown hair is piled in a messy bun on top of her head. A blast of deliciously cold air hits me as she rolls down the window.

"Hi," I say tentatively, peering inside. She wears cut-off jeans and a Yale T-shirt and doesn't look particularly threatening.

"Well, you're a hot mess," she says, giving me the once-over. "What happened?"

"I got in a fight with my best friend," I lie, "and, well, she kind of kicked me out of the car, and . . ."

My new friend holds up her hand. "Ugh. Best friends. I hear you. Where are you headed?"

When I tell her, she grins. "I'm headed that way! Aren't you *lucky*?"

Honestly, I would say my relationship with luck is on the fritz. We might even have broken up.

Chapter 17

MINIMISSION MADNESS.

MY FRIENDS AMBUSH the red Honda before it even clears the gates. They drag me from the car, barely giving me time to thank my rescuer.

"What happened?" Charlotte demands. "Who was that? What's going on?"

Izumi pulls me into an uncharacteristic hug, squeezing the air right out of my lungs. "The car service couldn't find you," she whispers. "We thought you were *dead*."

I hug her back. "I'm sorry. The phone died. I used the snarling dog."

Toby eyes me. "And?"

"I was kidnapped," I say.

"I meant snarling dog. How did it work?"

"Oh. Worked great." Toby grins. He loves real-world verification that his crazy apps work, even if getting such information requires perilous situations for others.

"I'm glad," he says. "Now give it back." He holds out his hand for the gold phone.

I pull it from my shorts. "Here's the thing," I say. "I broke it."

"Already?" he yells. "Abby!"

"I was being chased."

"You are *always* being chased!" He's very loud. People are staring. But he's right. It happens a lot. I'm not proud.

"Details, please," Izumi says, arms crossed defensively against her chest. But there are too many people here. And, possibly, butterflies.

"Let's get out of here," I say. "I can fill you in and we can call Jennifer."

We cut through the administrative building and head down to the lake, where things are quiet. The old rowboat we choose wobbles and tilts, threatening to dump us in the green water. It takes a few minutes to get our rowing rhythm down. Only when we are out in the middle do I feel like it's safe to talk.

"We know Baldy and Jane Ann are trading Team OP secrets to the Ghost for future Challenge victories," I begin. "We don't know what those secrets are, but we know they haven't gotten them yet."

"What could Poppy have come up with that has everyone freaking out?" Toby wonders. "And *how* did the Ghost get wind of it?"

"Wait. There's more. Tinker Bell is watching Baldy, hoping he'll lead her to the Ghost. When I showed up, she grabbed me."

"Tinker Bell?" Izumi asks, indignant.

"I know!"

"Are *all* the bad people from our past going to come back to haunt us?" Charlotte inquires.

"I really hope not," Toby says.

Bobbing quietly on the water, we think about the stakes. Just yesterday it was Jane Ann cheating. Today, it's something much more. But what exactly? Toby hands me the cracked phone, Jennifer's number already dialed.

"If you drop it in the lake," he says, "there is no telling what I will do to you."

"Hello? Hello?" It sounds like a hurricane. I can barely hear Jennifer's voice.

"Mom?"

"Abby? I'm in the middle of a hurricane." Of course, she is. "And this boat! Do *not* get me started. Who sets out on an ocean voyage without enough coffee?" *Uh-oh. Those pirates are going to rue the day they denied Jennifer Hunter her morning coffee.* "But enough about that. What's going on? Oh, boy. Hold on." In the background, I hear violent barfing. "Jasper! Cut that out! We have work to do! No time for seasickness! Abby? Can you believe I'm stuck with a first mate who suffers from motion sickness? Ridiculous!"

Toby's eyes glisten. "Is she really the captain of a pirate ship?" he whispers. I've learned it's best not to underestimate Jennifer Hunter. There's a mess of static interrupted by the sound of my mother in a high state of annoyance.

"No!" she yells. "I said *raise* the anchor, you idiot! Abby? Please remind me never to work with pirates again. They have not demonstrated the capacity to learn. Now, tell me how it goes with the water theme. Not that I especially *want* to talk about water. All I can see is water."

I quickly tell her the story, starting with the butterflies and ending with the museum. I leave out the bit about Tinker Bell because that will take too much time to explain. If Jennifer is shocked by my story, she does not show it.

"Interesting," she muses. "I guess I'd better get back there and deal with this ASAP."

These are the best words I have ever heard. But before I can tell her, there's a crash in the background followed by Jennifer cursing like a pirate. She's got it down perfectly.

"Where was I?" she continues. "Oh, yes. Coming to Briar. Let's see. Right now, I'm in the middle of the ocean, more or less. It might take me a few days to get to Hartford. So how shall we manage this? How about you and your friends keep tabs on Poppy in the meantime? And keep it quiet. I don't need a panicky teen on my hands. Just make sure she doesn't disappear suddenly." This makes my throat dry. "Let's consider it a minimission for the Center, but between us. If Mrs. Smith finds out, well, she's a bit overzealous where the Challenge is concerned, and she's likely to blow in there, guns blazing, and we'll miss an opportunity to see what our friend the Ghost is up to. What do you say?"

A minimission? For the Center? She can do *that*? I fist-pump the air a bunch of times and almost overturn our boat. "We say yes!"

"We do?" asks Toby. "To what?" I wave him off so I can hear Jennifer.

"Just don't do anything crazy," she says. "Keep your eyes open. Watch Poppy. Wait for me."

I agree, wish her luck with the pirates, and hang up. My friends eyeball me.

"We have a mission!" I shout.

And then I really do flip the boat over.

Chapter 18

DO MORE. DO BETTER.

IZUMI IS THE FIRST ONE to suggest that sitting around watching Poppy is not the best use of our skills. We have an afternoon and a night before the next Challenge task. Shouldn't we use it to, I don't know, find out what is so awesome about Poppy's ideas that an international, notorious, really *bad* bad guy is after them?

Wait a minute. Izumi is the one usually talking us back from the cliff's edge. It must be sleep deprivation muddling her brain. But her reasoning is sound.

"Look at it this way," she says as we lounge on the dock, hoping for a breeze. "Jennifer is still on the ocean. Even she can't move at the speed of light, so it will be at least a day or two until she gets here."

"Where are you going with this?" Toby asks, eyebrows furrowing with suspicion.

"Hear me out," she says. "Our mission is to keep an eye on Team OP and make sure the Ghost doesn't get what he wants from them. Right?"

Charlotte glances at me, as shocked as I am at this interpretation of our mission. It's the kind of stretch I usually go for. But Izumi? No way.

"Go on," I say.

"So isn't it our responsibility, our duty, to figure out what the Ghost wants?"

Toby's jaw drops. "Izumi! What is wrong with you?"

She grins. "I have no idea! Maybe I'm exhausted? I feel a little weird."

"Or maybe," says Charlotte, "you're exactly right. It's our duty as temporary Center agents to get the goods."

"That is *not* what Jennifer said," Toby says, shaking his head, resigned.

"So what's the plan?" Charlotte asks. They all look at me. Why do they look at me?

"We need to get into Poppy's room," I say, because that seems a logical first step. "And her computer."

"Why don't we just ask her?" Toby suggests.

"Because she will just run to Mrs. Smith," I say. "And we're not supposed to tell her."

"We're not supposed to be looking for the thing the Ghost is looking for, either," Toby says hotly.

"We're just doing a little poking around, that's all," I say, hoping to ease his mind.

"Famous last words," Toby groans. "This is how it *always* starts with you guys."

After some debate, which includes lots of eye-rolling from Toby, we decide that Poppy's idea book is the place to start our not-quite-sanctioned investigation. I'm dispatched to the game room to see if I can find Poppy and somehow steal her notebook without her noticing. Poppy is not there, but Owen Elliott is, glassy-eyed and muttering at the Asteroids machine, fingers frantic on the big white buttons.

"Hey," I say.

"Go away," he says sharply. "I'm concentrating."

I take a step back, surprised by his tone. "You're almost at high score," I say.

"I *know*. And if you go away, I might get it."

"How long have you been playing?" I ask.

"Since after lunch," Owen Elliott says. No wonder he

looks insane. That's almost five hours. Does he take bathroom breaks? "When you were supposed to *meet* me."

Oh, *no*. I do a mental facepalm. I was stalking Baldy when I was supposed to be getting my Asteroids tutorial. "I'm really sorry," I say quickly. "I just . . . um . . . something came up."

"Sure it did."

I've hurt his feelings. What am I supposed to do now? "Can we play later?" I ask. He gives me a half-hearted shrug that I take as an invitation to please get lost. "Where's Poppy?" I can't steal her notebook if I don't know where she is. Feeling bad for blowing off Owen Elliott will have to wait.

"At the pool," he says.

"Swimming?"

"No," he replies with a withering look. "Playing tennis."

Okay. I deserved that. But you can't take a notebook in the water with you! "Gotta go!" I say quickly.

My friends meet me at the aquatics center, on the far side of campus. By the time I get there, I have the backbone of a plan. Izumi will hop in the pool and challenge Poppy to a race. Poppy, being competitive, will not be able to resist. Meanwhile, Charlotte and I will sneak into the locker room and photograph the notebook with Toby's new *red* spy phone. Does he just conjure these phones out of the air? I mean, how many does he *have*? He didn't say what will happen to me if I damage it because he did not have to. Begrudgingly, he takes up his station outside the locker room entrance, ready to alert us if Poppy gets out of the pool. As plans go, it's pretty good. I wonder if Jane Ann has already looked at the notebook and didn't find the thing she was looking for. Either that, or she doesn't know it exists. I hope we don't bump into each other.

But the pool locker room is empty and just about as steamy as it is outdoors.

"Which one?" asks Charlotte, staring at the rows and rows of brightly painted lockers.

Good question. Our plan did not include that level of detail. It never does. "She wears those white Keds," I say. "The ones with the stripes." As we get down low to peer under the benches, searching for Poppy's footwear, the red spy phone falls from my pocket and into a puddle.

"No!" *Oh, please let Toby have waterproofed it!* I grab it up and wipe it on my shorts, just in time for Charlotte to call me over. She points to white Keds nestled under locker number forty-seven.

"Check it out," she says.

"Perfect. Now how do we get in the locker?"

Charlotte gives me an arched eyebrow and, without a word, hip-checks the long, slim locker so hard I think I hear a *crack*. But she just grins as the door pops open. "These lockers are lame," she says.

"Nice," I say with admiration. We dig through Poppy's stuff, careful not to let anything fall on the wet floor. At the bottom, under her Smith-issued uniform shirt is the notebook. Quickly, I pull out the slightly damp, cracked phone and begin madly flipping pages and photographing the contents. Her handwriting is disgustingly perfect, and her little illustrations could be in a real book. Maybe Poppy should think about leaving something for the rest of us to do well?

I'm about halfway through when we hear Toby outside the door. "Hack. Cough. Sneeze. She's coming! Sneeze. Hack."

"Hurry," whispers. Charlotte. "I'll run defense."

Sure enough, here comes Poppy, fresh off a crushing defeat at the hands of Izumi and plenty annoyed by it. "Her strokes are not even good," she mutters to herself. "And all that splashing! She might be a rugby star, but she has a few things to learn about swimming."

"She beat you," says another girl.

"She was *fresh*," Poppy counters. "I'd been swimming for at least a half hour already."

"Whatever," says the girl, peeling off into another section of locker room. I'm almost done. A few more pages.

"Poppy," I hear Charlotte say, her voice dripping honey. "I *love* your suit. Where did you get it?"

"It's the Smith school uniform," Poppy says. "Why are you in here?"

"Oh, just, you know, waiting for Izumi."

"She's got about five girls lined up to race her," snarls Poppy. "She's going to be a while."

"Did you lose?" asks Charlotte sweetly. I flip to the last page and snap a photo. "By a lot? By entire seconds? I'm dying to know!"

"Get out of my way," Poppy responds. "Please."

"Be careful!" Charlotte warns. "The floor is wet."

I hear a loud *thud*. "Ouch!"

"I told you to watch out for that puddle," Charlotte chides.

"You did that on purpose!" complains Poppy.

Uh-oh. Quickly, I stuff everything back in the locker and jam it shut with my shoulder. As it slams, a flash of shimmery blue and yellow, *butterfly* colors, catches the corner of my eye. But when I look again, there's nothing. Now I'm hallucinating insects.

"Let me help you up," offers Charlotte.

"No! Stay away from me."

"Okay. Have it your way."

I come around the corner with a grin plastered to my face, my heart racing. "What are you doing on the floor, Poppy? Oh, there you are, Charlotte. We better get back out there so we can cheer on Izumi. Poppy, you want to join us?"

She doesn't answer, just glares at me. The phone is warm in my back pocket. Toby has got to do something about how his new spy phones heat up before someone burns herself. I grab Charlotte by the arm. "Let's *go*."

We dash out of the locker room, leaving a disgruntled Poppy in our wake.

Chapter 19

WITS.

AN HOUR LATER, we cram into the auditorium for the announcement of Challenge task number two. Izumi's hair is still wet. The smell of nervous sweat permeates the air. The Briar team surfs in on the wave of their first win. Statistically, the rest of us are in an uphill battle.

We sit five rows back from the stage. Toby's head is bent over the red phone, patiently uploading the photographs of the notebook to his personal network, where his software will analyze them. Does it look for phrases like *world ending* or *likely to cause Armageddon*? I know better than to ask. Instead, I wring my damp hands together in my lap and stare at him. Every few seconds he throws me a dirty look, meaning I should cut it out, but I can't help it. I want to know what is in those photographs.

Jane Ann is in her usual seat, twirling a length of shiny hair around her finger. She seems relaxed, but Baldy has big sweaty half-moons under his armpits. As he steps up to the microphone, anxiety comes off him in waves. I get it. Angering the Ghost is not the recipe for a long and healthy life. He gives us a weak smile and clears his throat.

"Resourcefulness," he begins, eyes flicking around like a disco ball. "Inventiveness. Gumption. Cleverness. The Glass sisters did not believe simply being smart in the classroom was enough. They wanted Challengers to prove they could navigate the real world. Find resources. Make connections. Succeed without being led. And that is why the second Challenge task is all about using your wits."

A few dozen students start a low chant of "smarts, wits, pressure, smarts, wits, pressure." Baldy holds up his hand for silence. "Our theme is water. So far, each team has produced a device to provide clean water to people who don't have any. Now it's time to take it to the next level. Each team will be given an envelope containing a clue, the name of a destination, and the means to get there. Once you arrive, it is up to you to decipher the clue and find the person, place, or thing that will help your team maximize the benefit of your invention. Find a place willing to manufacture it for cheap. Discover a way to distribute your invention globally. Get a few minutes with an expert who can help you improve your invention. Do all of the above. The choice is yours. Make it wisely."

Murmurs ripple through the crowd. For a wits task, this is not bad. Veronica's year, the theme was global warming. All the teams were dumped in a random Canadian forest with an orange and a pencil and told to find their way out. I guess the judges wanted them to have intimate knowledge of nature. Of course, thinking something is going to be simple is what happens right before everything becomes super complicated.

"The wits task kicks off at seven o'clock tomorrow morning in the auditorium," Baldy says. "I recommend a good night's sleep and a protein-heavy breakfast. Gemma and Emma Glass were fond of saying, 'You have wits, now use them.' I will leave you with that." Baldy hurries off the stage, using the rear exit to avoid being cornered by stressed-out teams hoping for a morsel of information that will put them ahead.

Outside, the sun sinks lower in the sky but the heat persists. The air is still, and little flies circle our heads incessantly. But they are way too small to be drones. At least I think they are? All flying bugs and insects are now suspicious. Suddenly, a wave of fatigue threatens to drown me. This has been the longest day of my life. I can't even remember when it started.

"Are the photos done?" I ask.

Toby glances at his phone. "Two hours," Toby replies. "After dinner. In the meantime, I want to show you guys something." He slings his bulging backpack up over his shoulder. "Come on."

He heads down the path to the lake and out to a dense crop of trees that reach right to the shoreline. The crickets begin to hum. My stomach growls.

"What's with the nature walk?" Charlotte asks after a while.

Toby stops and faces us. "Things have changed," he says.

"You mean because of the Ghost?" Izumi whispers, as if saying the name too loudly will conjure the man himself.

"Yes. Last time we weren't prepared. I don't want that to happen again." From his pack, he pulls a bag of individually wrapped caramels, rainbow shoelaces, and Smith School baseball hats.

"Are you running away?" I ask.

"No," he says shortly. "I'm helping to save *you*, as usual."

I resent the implication. Sometimes I save myself. And others.

Charlotte digs into the pile. Toby swats her hand away and suddenly I get it. Mrs. Smith might have kicked him off spy-gadget duty, but that has not stopped him from creating them anyway.

"You did *not*," I say.

He grins. "I did."

"Show us."

"What's going on?" Izumi interrupts.

"Spy gadgets," I say.

"Oh, wow," she says. "For us?"

"Now, they aren't, like, Angus level," Toby explains, referring to the gadget and gear master at the spy college. "There are some quirks. But none that are deadly. I don't think so, anyway. Beta testing is difficult when you can't exactly *tell* anyone what you're doing."

The rainbow laces are accelerant for the candy, which explodes. Toby pinches off a piece of shoelace, wraps it around a caramel, and throws it at a tree. It takes all four of us jumping around like lunatics to put out the sparks. The tree, black with soot, will never forgive us. My ears ring.

"What do the hats do?" Charlotte asks, perching one on her head just so.

"They provide protection for when you use these." From his backpack, he pulls three sleek silver smartphones. *Spy phones*.

Izumi gasps. "Are those what I think they are?" she asks.

Toby nods solemnly. "But don't get too excited," he says. "They only have a few defensive apps." Charlotte grabs one and immediately starts tapping.

"Stop!" Toby yelps. "You're going to hurt someone!"

"Isn't that the point?"

"No," we say.

"Then why are you giving me exploding shoelaces?"

"The point of all of this stuff is to *buy time*," Toby says. "Abby knows." Do I ever. Extra seconds can make the difference between escape and failure. Charlotte looks disappointed.

"Now, I've improved the functionality in these devices," Toby says, cradling a silver baby in his hands. "They are calibrated to your voices and faces."

"Can we play solitaire?" Izumi asks with a sly smile.

Toby glares at her. "Not funny. Demo time. Put on your hats." We don the Smith caps and wait while Toby taps the phone. "This one is the *best*. Blaring horn. I love it!" We wait. Nothing happens. We wait some more. Toby grins.

"Um, does it actually do anything?" I ask, just as a bird falls out of the sky and lands on my head. Naturally, I scream.

"You can't kill birds!" Izumi howls.

Toby scrambles to explain. "It's not dead, just dazed. The hats protect you from the high-pitched frequency. Don't use it without the hat or you will knock yourself out." After thirty seconds, the bird hops to its feet, gives us a dirty look, and launches into the sky. I wait for it to poop on Toby's head, but it doesn't.

"What else?" Charlotte asks, eyes bright. "What about the bees?"

The bees spray a flurry of hard glass beads, simulating what it feels like being attacked by a swarm.

"How about the lightning?" I ask.

"It can shatter glass. Just hold the phone against it and it breaks apart. I like that one too. And you already know about the snarling dog."

"Why is the Cookie app on here?" I ask. Unlike on the gold phone, here it is blurred out.

"It's just an image," he says. "I didn't have time to remove it, but don't worry, it doesn't work. There is nothing behind it."

"Anything else we should know?" I ask. I love this

phone. True, I love them all, but this one is especially awesome.

"Battery life is a problem," he says. "I'm working on a fix, but who has time? School is really getting in the way of my progress."

Izumi says what we are all thinking. "Are you kidding me? Toby, you're a genius." He blushes and stares at his feet.

"No big deal," he says. "Please don't wreck them. Abby. Okay?"

Toby would like an oath sworn in blood, but he will have to make due with our promises. We load up our new gear, reverently, carefully. Toby has gone beyond the call of duty.

On the walk back to the dorms, everyone is quiet. It's like we've taken our relationship to the next level by exchanging spy gear. Whatever happens next, we are in this together.

Chapter 20

OWEN ELLIOTT FORGIVES ME.

OWEN ELLIOTT TEXTS ME to see if I will meet him at the docks. I am zombie-level tired and want nothing more than to eat and sleep and wait for Toby to say the photos analysis is done. But maybe Owen Elliott wants to forgive me for blowing him off? That possibility feels surprisingly good, enough so I pull my shoes back on and traipse out the door.

The campus is dotted with kids playing Frisbee and hacky sack, lounging under shade trees and listening to music. The really smart kids, it seems, are the ones who *didn't* enter the Challenge. They're just hanging out and having fun. I crest a small rise and head down to the docks.

But he's not there. I sit on the dock to wait. Ten minutes later, still no Owen Elliott. Is he getting back at me for leaving him stranded in the game room? That's cheap.

I wait a little longer just in case he was held hostage by Poppy for some reason, but he doesn't show up. Well, forget it. I'm out of here. A crescendo of cricket song rises as the sun drops. The pathway lights flicker on. I indulge in a fantasy of my head on a soft, cool pillow, eyes closed, dreaming of victory. The mere idea of bed makes me sigh with pleasure.

I'm so lost in this thought that I don't notice someone is behind me until it's too late. In a flash, I'm facedown in the grass, the wind knocked from my lungs, a knee digging into my spine. An involuntary groan escapes my lips. Am I really being mugged on the Briar Academy campus? For what? I'm not even wearing my cool tennis shoes because the right one is still in Tinker Bell's car.

Veronica says that when you are in a dangerous situation, the first thing you must do is clear your mind, create a blank space where you can envision your actions. I try that. My blank space immediately fills with fury toward Owen Elliott for *setting me up*. Did he tell Poppy I blew him off and she decided to demonstrate some of her black-belt karate skills on me? Veronica also says your action should never come from a place of fear or anger. Whatever.

I manage to get my palms flat on the ground. The move is called Camel, and it's one of Veronica's favorites. I clench my abs and shoot my butt up in the air, using my arms for leverage. The idea is to toss the attacker off my back. Despite my still-strong biceps, it doesn't work. Whoever it is hangs on and goes for my shorts pockets. The spy phone!

Toby has forgiven me for a lot, but if this silver beauty gets stolen, I'm done for. He will never trust me again. I press my hips to the dirt, feeling the hard outline of the phone dig into my skin. The person grabs my hair and pulls my head back, twisting my neck at an unnatural angle. I swing my arm around and get a piece of T-shirt. Hair brushes my hand. A long ponytail. Poppy hair.

Did she see me in the locker room photographing her book? Did she overhear Toby telling us about the spy phones, and she can't imagine anyone inventing something cooler than what she's invented? Come to think of it, there are many reasons why Poppy might want to beat me up.

There's another thing Veronica taught me. It's called the Crow, and you use the sharp end of your elbow to jab your opponent in the eye. It can be painful and effective. I've never tried it while pinned down, but I'm willing to give it a go. I roll to the left for leverage and hammer my elbow up into my assailant. I miss her eye but get her square in the nose. She yelps. It's probably bleeding. This is my opportunity. While she's distracted, I heave her off my back with a wild Camel. She tumbles into the grass, into the darkness. All I can make out is the silver phone, which she waves at me before breaking into a run.

No. Way. I leap to my feet and sprint after her toward the woods on the edge of campus. But she does that seven-minute mile. My muscles burn. I should take exercise more seriously. Izumi would have tackled her already. My breath comes in hot, choking gasps. In thirty seconds, I will definitely collapse.

But Poppy trips on a branch hidden by leaves, sprawling face-first into the ground. The phone flies out of her hand. I love nature! Leaping over her, I grab the phone. She gets me by the ankle, her nails digging half-moons into my flesh. I kick her off and roll away. On all fours, she pursues like a half-crazed dog. Fighting in the dense woods in the dark is not a scenario Veronica ever envisioned in her training sessions, which makes me a little sad. I scramble to my feet. Poppy pulls me down.

And we're back where we started. I'm pinned to the

ground, my mouth full of pretty autumn leaves. A rock digs into my jawbone. I clutch the phone in my hand while Poppy squeezes my wrist, intent on getting me to drop it. And suddenly, there it is, the blank space Veronica talked about. My head goes quiet. I see the scene as if from above. As much as it infuriates me, I am no match for Poppy in these conditions. She wants the phone and she will get it.

But I am not going to let that happen.

I bring the phone down hard on the rock beside my head. It pops and shatters. I smash it again and again, little slivers of glass embedding in my palm. "There," I wheeze. "Now you can have it."

Poppy growls, her prize in shards, and she takes off into the woods. Abby one, Poppy zero. I sit on the forest floor collecting my thoughts and the bits and pieces of the beautiful silver spy phone.

Toby is going to be really mad.

Chapter 21

HOW LOW WILL THEY GO?

MY FRIENDS ARE STUNNED that Poppy would sink so low. I can't decide if I'm madder at Poppy or Owen Elliott for setting me up.

"As of this moment," I announce, "Owen Elliott is dead to me." The experience has left me stuck between embarrassed and furious. My friends swear he likes me, but is this the way you treat somebody you like? To make matters worse, Poppy almost got the better of me. Overall, not my best experience.

Toby sifts through the pieces of smashed spy phone on his dinner tray. "It took you less than two hours," he says, shocked.

Come on, Toby, it's not like I killed your secret cat or anything. I had no choice, not being stronger or better or more *extraordinary*. Quietly, Toby packs up the pieces. "I'll let you guys know about the photographs," he says glumly, leaving us to our macaroni and cheese.

As a reward for not *actually* losing the phone or *actually* getting beat, I treat myself to three bowls of mint chip ice cream, covered in heaps of whipped cream and those horrifying red cherries Jennifer never lets me have. It works wonders.

I fall asleep before my head hits the pillow and don't move a muscle until Izumi shakes me awake at six o'clock the next morning.

"Time for breakfast," she says, much too chipper for the early hour. "And time to test our wits. Plus, Toby has news."

This should get me going, but my legs feel like lead and my head swims and it takes Izumi physically dragging me out of bed to wake me up. Good thing she's strong. She throws some clothes at me and stands guard until I put them on and brush my teeth. She does not trust that I won't sneak back to bed.

But if I'm bad, Toby is far worse. He sags over his breakfast like a plant dying of thirst. "Long night," he mumbles. "Bad data."

"What happened?" Izumi asks. "What's in the book?"

"I don't know," Toby says defensively. "The images were blurry, like *wet*, or something."

Oops. That might be my fault. "I have no idea how that happened," I say.

"It will take longer for the program to find anything useful from them," Toby adds, with a sigh.

"It's almost seven," I say. "We should make sure we are on time to get our wits clue."

But in the auditorium, we find a stranger up onstage rather than Baldy. Rumors fly around his absence. Baldy was mauled by a bear. He was bit by a viper. He fell out of a rowboat and drowned. He got food poisoning. He was arrested for embezzling money from the school. He got a really good deal on airline tickets to Italy, so he took a quick vacation. The stranger onstage, sweating through his pink button-down shirt, is Baldy's assistant, a young man with round glasses and wispy hair. He taps the microphone a few times to get our attention.

"Students," he says. His voice is thin and reedy. "May I have your attention? Attention, please!"

"Where's the headmaster?" someone shouts.

The assistant wrings his hands. "I'm sorry, but the headmaster has been . . . detained. I've been instructed to carry on in his place." Baldy is gone? I glance over my shoulder to the seat where Jane Ann always sits. It's empty. If my palms weren't already sweaty, they would be now. This can only mean one thing—the Ghost ran out of patience.

"This is bad," Charlotte whispers.

"Seriously," Izumi agrees.

Yeah. And if the Ghost ran out of patience with Baldy and Jane Ann, he is probably right now plotting another way to get what he wants from Team OP. But the Ghost never does his own dirty work. My eyes dart around the auditorium looking for anyone suspicious, but it's just confused-looking teams.

Onstage, Baldy's assistant fumbles with a large envelope tucked under his arm. "I have here your clues, as discussed yesterday. Please retrieve them as you leave the auditorium."

As the teams press toward the exit, we stay seated, unsettled. Jennifer is nowhere to be found, and we have to make a choice: participate in the wits task like a nice, normal Challenge team or keep to our Center minimission and follow Poppy. We all know what it means.

"Left or right," mutters Toby.

"Rock and a hard place," adds Izumi.

"Scylla and Charybdis," Charlotte whispers.

"Yeah," I add. "But I'll do whatever you guys want to do."

Toby looks at me, surprised. "Really?"

"Yes." In my heart, I want to follow Poppy. I want to prove I can be trusted to do as I'm told, to follow orders even at great personal sacrifice. But I want my friends to want that too.

Toby shakes his head sadly. He's going to say we have to complete the Challenge task. But instead, he says, "Center missions take priority over everything. It's what Mrs. Smith drilled into us when I used to, um, work for her. We have to follow Poppy."

"Statistically, we can't win anyway," Izumi adds thoughtfully. "So we might as well go ahead and save the world our way."

I do not point out that we have no plan for what to do if the Ghost makes a move to kidnap Poppy or something equally awful. We don't discuss how unlikely it is for four kids to defeat a criminal mastermind intent on getting what he wants. No one mentions how much trouble we could be in if all we do is make a bad situation worse.

But here's the thing. Izumi, Charlotte, Toby, me— we've weighed the risks, we know the odds, and we willingly accept them. The four of us want the same thing, and we want it for one another, and we want to get it together.

This is what being a team is all about.

Chapter 22

THE BLUE WHALE.

THE TEAMS GATHER OUTSIDE the auditorium as white envelopes containing clues are distributed. Ours contains a photo of Grand Central Terminal in New York City and train tickets.

Charlotte bounces up and down on her heels. "A mission," she says, eyes bright. "I love it."

"A minimission," Toby clarifies.

"But we will get credit with the Center for doing our job, right?" Izumi asks.

"Of course," I say. *Won't we?*

"I hate to break it to you," interrupts Izumi, "but Team OP is going to be out of here in a second, and we should probably know where they are headed if we intend to follow them."

"Ideas?" I ask. We're in a crowd, surrounded by people. Our options are limited.

"Follow my lead," Charlotte whispers. We edge close to Team OP. Poppy holds the clue. Owen Elliott looks over her shoulder, nodding and scowling.

"Abby," Charlotte commands. "Stand right here. Just like that. Okay, perfect." With that, she gives me a mighty shove right into Poppy. Before I can protest, we are down in a heap. Charlotte rushes to our aid.

"Are you okay?" she asks. "Oh man, what happened? Poppy, you keep falling down! Look at your elbow!"

There's a small scratch, but from her reaction you'd think she lost ten gallons of blood. Horrified, she drops the clue. "I'm injured!" she howls as Owen Elliott swoops in to help. "And it's all your fault!" She glares daggers at me while Charlotte gracefully scoops up the clue and passes it back to Toby, who photographs it and tosses it back to the ground at Poppy's feet. They are so smooth it's like ballet. I untangle from Poppy, who's on the verge of hysteria because she scraped her elbow.

"I'm sorry," I say. "I tripped."

Poppy has tears in her eyes, and her lower lip trembles.

"It really hurts," she moans. "You ruin everything."

I ruin everything? How dare she? "You tried to steal my phone," I bark. "You attacked me in the woods!"

Genuine confusion flashes across her face. "You're insane," she says. "But *that's* not a surprise."

"Abby," Toby chides. "Come *on*." Poppy shoots me a series of world-class dirty looks as Toby drags me away. The teams disperse, buzzing about their next moves. I squeeze in next to Charlotte for a better view of the photo Toby snapped of Team OP's clue. It's a photo of a whale.

"The Museum of Natural History," I say. "It's the blue whale model." I'm appalled by their blank looks. "How can you not know the blue whale? She's twenty-one thousand pounds, ninety-four feet long, and a replica of an actual whale found in 1925 off the coast of South America."

Toby gives me a curious look. "You have a weird knowledge base," he says.

"What's *weird* is that you have never seen the blue whale," I counter.

"At least our train tickets will get us there," Charlotte points out. "And just in time. I grow weary of this preppy paradise." We fall in behind Team OP, subtly I hope, as a big group trudges toward the train station. The game is *on*.

There are at least ten teams here waiting for the train

to New York City, which helps us not stand out. In minutes, a city-bound train glides into the station. When the doors open, a gaggle of unchaperoned students tumble on, much to the horror of the regular commuters. Team OP climbs on the first car while we board car number two in time to claim the last seats, directly across the aisle from the toilet. Gross.

Suddenly, Toby's phone starts merrily chirping. His eyes, already at half-mast as the train rocks us gently, fly open. "It must be done," he whispers. The red spy phone glows. We lean in for a closer look as Toby scrolls through a document with tiny print.

"Interesting," he murmurs. "Really? She can do that? I didn't think it was possible."

Charlotte whacks him on the head with an open palm. "Tell us!"

"Ouch! Jeez. It looks like there are a few ideas that she has come up with that are pretty cool."

"Like, cool enough for the Ghost to want to steal?"

"Possibly. Look at this." He holds the phone up, zooming in on a slightly blurry patch of Poppy's loopy handwriting and a sketch. "It's the details on Blackout."

"That program that can mess with your electronics?"

"Yeah. It can infiltrate your house or your dorm room

through whatever electronics you have—laptop, phone, television, a smart hub like Alexa or Siri, even your refrigerator if it's wired. And then it can control your house. Like turn off the music, turn on the lights, run the heat, start your car, open your garage. You know, become the brain of your house. Or dorm room. Or wherever."

"But hasn't this been done before?" Izumi asks. "What's the big deal?"

"It's been done," Toby replies, "but her solution, if it works, is incredibly simple, even a little beautiful." He sounds impressed, dazzled, and this rarely happens. "The Ghost could use Blackout to take control of things like electricity and power in a heartbeat. He could turn off this train or the network that controls all the trains. Or crash a bunch of airplanes into the ground or one another. Or plunge us into darkness. Basically, he could hold the country hostage. It's a recipe for chaos."

We let this settle in. The Ghost, able to turn the country off and on at will, does not sound good. "Is there more?" I ask, dreading the answer.

"A lot more," Toby says, "like smart fabric that tells you if you sweat too much or are too cold or getting sick, but that doesn't seem to have world-ending implications, right? Blackout seems more potentially sinister."

The train lurches into a new station. Two men in black jackets and sunglasses climb aboard our car. There is nothing inherently suspicious about them, but the little hairs on my arms stand at attention. They take a seat a few rows ahead of us. Everyone is now suspect.

"I guess it's good we're keeping an eye on her then," Charlotte says quietly. "Let's not mess it up." But within five minutes they are all asleep. So much for eagle-eyed spies. The train trundles lazily toward New York City. Outside the window, the landscape turns gray and urban, and the trees disappear.

My friends sleep hard, Izumi muttering about the weather, Toby drooling on his shirt. I eat brownies lifted from the cafeteria. Briar has its problems, clearly, but their food is delicious. After an hour, Toby wakes up. He stares at the crumbs on my T-shirt.

"Did you save me any?" he asks.

"No."

"Thanks."

"Sorry."

He rubs the sleep out of his eyes and stretches his arms above his head. "I have something for you," he says.

"More brownies?"

He digs into his pack and pulls out the gold spy phone,

the one I broke running from Tinker Bell. "This is the only phone I have left," he says. "I fixed the screen."

A lump in my throat almost keeps me from answering. "I'm really sorry about the silver one."

He gives me a funny look. "If you were a cat, you'd be on life number eight or something by now."

I mumble promises about keeping the phone safe, putting life number eight on the line if necessary, but Toby just grunts and goes back to his nap. The men in the black jackets don't sleep. They don't talk. They don't read. They maintain perfect posture. Definitely suspicious. No one can sit for this long without slouching.

Finally, we rumble into Grand Central Terminal. Somewhere in this building is a person or thing that can help us take our water-cleaning device to the next level. But we will never know what it is because we have chosen our mission to follow Poppy over the Challenge wits task.

Jennifer once dragged me to Miami in August to meet a man she called an "old friend." This was before I knew she was a spy and that all these "old friends" were actually contacts giving her information. She said this particular "old friend" was a brilliant scientist and could have used his ability to cure diseases and stuff, but instead he went a different direction and did some things that haunted him to this day. It seemed to bum her out. I remember wondering why she'd come all this way, with me in tow, to hang out with a guy she clearly didn't like.

But what she was really talking about was *choice*, taking a left instead of a right, going forward instead of back. Every time we decide to do something, one avenue shuts down and another opens up. And you can't return to the one you rejected. Today, we've decided to lose the Challenge in favor of potentially keeping a dangerous weapon out of the hands of a madman.

And we can't go back.

Chapter 23

PRESSURE.

I ROUSE MY TEAM, something they are not thrilled about, and point out the window. "We're here," I say. "Wake up."

As we exit to a perfume of old cabbage, fuel, and pee, I keep one eye on Team OP and the other on the men in black jackets. How can Poppy not notice them? And how can a girl who doesn't notice them be in line for early admittance to spy school?

We stream out of Grand Central right into the middle of bustling midtown Manhattan. The sidewalks teem with glassy-eyed, sunburned tourists speaking dozens of languages. For an anxious moment, we lose Team OP in a gaggle of rowdy uniformed school kids who spread to the sidewalk edge like spilled milk.

And the men in black jackets vanish. I scan the crowd, but there is no sign of them. It's possible they are just two guys with good posture and matching clothes. Finally, we get eyes on Poppy and Owen Elliott. Deep depression sets in when we realize they plan on walking the 2.2 miles to the American Museum of Natural History.

"Take the subway!" Charlotte screams. "Or a cab. Or Lyft. Or fly on a freaking unicorn! I don't care. Just no walking. It's too hot!"

But they walk, so we walk.

And we complain. Actually, mostly Charlotte complains. "The first true automobile was invented in 1886," she huffs. "And since that time, humans have ridden in them to avoid the discomfort of walking in four-hundred-degree heat."

As I recall, the last time we were in New York City together, it was freezing, and she didn't like that, either. Poppy moves fast, seemingly unfazed by the crowds or the melting sidewalks. Owen Elliott struggles to keep up.

We blaze down Fifth Avenue. Frosty air escapes the doors of trendy boutiques, embracing us. I almost swoon. Poppy doesn't notice. She breaks left into Central Park, skirting the Central Park Zoo, charging hard toward the museum. She never once glances over her shoulder to see if Owen is keeping up. It's almost as if she doesn't care. I wonder if disregard for one's teammates is something Mrs. Smith finds attractive in a potential spy?

When we finally roll up at the museum entrance off Central Park West, we are hot and perilously close to grumpy.

"Saving the world is not worth this," Charlotte groans as she wipes sweat from her brow.

"I won't argue that," Izumi agrees.

"They just went in," I say quickly. "We need tickets."

Toby holds up his phone. "Got them." We enter the museum, but Team OP is nowhere in sight.

"To the whale," I say.

"You and that whale," Charlotte replies.

"It's cool," I say. "You'll see." We head for the Milstein Hall of Ocean Life, where the model blue whale is suspended from the ceiling. But to get there, we have to fight a tide of tourists, packed in shoulder to shoulder. This place sure is popular.

"We should be making salmon noises," Charlotte says as we battle through the bodies.

"I don't think salmon speak," responds Izumi.

In the Hall of Ocean Life, we find Team OP standing

under the enormous whale, looking perplexed. I scan the crowd for men in black jackets or other suspicious types, but all I see are people enjoying themselves. Except for Poppy and Owen Elliott. They argue. Poppy cannot see how something in this room will help improve her already-perfect water filtration device, and she's taking it out on Owen Elliott. After a moment of heated discussion, they storm off in opposite directions.

This, of course, is a complication.

"I'll take Poppy," I bark. "Toby, you're on Owen Elliott. Charlotte and Izumi, cover the main exits. Don't let them leave!"

Poppy finds the nearest elevator and descends into the bowels of the building. I race for the stairs, taking them two at a time and almost breaking both my legs, arriving moments after she exits the elevator car. She follows signs for the research library. The lower level is not crowded, so I hang back.

The museum's research library is intended for scholars, researchers, and other brainy people attempting to solve the many problems of our world. Through double glass doors, I spy a woman with buzz-cut purple hair and a pierced nose, sitting at a large desk. She chews gum and examines her phone. I stay hidden.

Purple, whose name tag I can't see, looks up as Poppy enters. She grins and blows a bubble so big her face disappears. Poppy introduces herself as a student participating in the Invitational Interschool Global Problems and Solutions Challenge and in need of assistance.

"The who?" asks Purple, smacking her gum loudly.

"It's a contest," Poppy says, impatiently, "for kids trying to make the world a better place. It's the wits task, and I need to be resourceful or I will lose. And I can't lose. That's unacceptable."

Purple stares at her. "I have absolutely no idea what you're talking about," she says.

Poppy taps her foot, impatient. One thing I've learned is that when it comes to spying, things rarely go as planned. You have to think on your feet. Evidence suggests Poppy is not good at this. Purple grins, amused by the foot tapping.

"It's a *contest*," Poppy says, slowly and loudly, as if this will help Purple get it. I can't wait to see where this goes, but before that happens, my recently acquired gold spy phone erupts in a chorus of *ping*s and *beep*s. Poppy glances over her shoulder just as I throw myself around the corner, out of sight. The small screen floods with a string of texts from my teammates.

Toby: *In Hall of Mammals. Two dudes talking to Owen. Might be guys from train?*

Charlotte: *Nothing at the exit. Oh, wait a minute. . . .*

Izumi: *Abby, where are you?*

Toby: *Don't . . .*

Charlotte: *Abby! They're . . .*

I don't even consider Poppy. I just run for the elevator, pulling up GPS tracking on my friends as I go. They're still in the museum, Toby under the blue whale, the girls by the exits. I elbow my way through the visitors, squaring my shoulders like I've seen commuters do when leaving the subway. A few people bounce off me and throw me dirty looks. There's no sign of Toby or Owen Elliott in Ocean Life. I skirt around an unruly school group and bolt for the nearest exit. A security guard yells at me for running, but I ignore him. No Izumi. An adrenaline spike sends my heart racing. Charlotte is gone too.

With shaking fingers, I pull up the tracker.

But the dots on the screen indicating where they are just spin and spin. My friends have disappeared.

Chapter 24

SMART FABRIC TO THE RESCUE.

I FIRE OFF A FEW FRANTIC TEXTS. Nothing comes back. Did the men in black jackets go for Owen Elliott? Did my friends end up as bycatch when they tried to protect him?

Think, Abby, think. I tuck the phone in my pocket and begin a systematic search of the enormous museum. After twenty minutes, I give up, my hands shaking with frustration. I call my mother, but she doesn't pick up.

"Come *on*, Mom!" I bark at the phone. "*Where* are you?" Having a mother for whom floating around the ocean with a bunch of pirates is not out of the ordinary can sometimes be a total pain.

What do I do? I've lost my friends before, and I've found them before. *Think*, Abby! True, I have no way of finding my team, or Owen Elliott, but maybe Poppy *does*. I have no choice but to ask.

I find her back under the blue whale, looking annoyed. She keeps checking her phone and indulging in exasperated sighs. She has no idea her teammate has been snatched from right under her nose. I don't care how good she looks on paper, she'd make a lousy spy. Finally, she wiggles into a small space on one of the benches and stares into space, her phone dangling from her hand. She seems a little lost, like the wind has gone out of her sails.

When I appear in front of her, she jumps from her seat as if ready to take me out with a swift uppercut. "What are *you* doing here?" she demands. "Are you stalking us? Trying to interfere so we don't win? I could *so* see you doing that. Don't you have your own wits task to manage?"

I take a step back. All she thinks about is herself, no matter the circumstances. If Poppy does end up in spy school, I *already* feel sorry for her partner. "Where is Owen Elliott?" I demand.

Bravado suddenly gone, her eyes flick nervously around. She glances at her phone. "He was supposed to meet me here, but he's not answering his texts. What did you do to him?"

"Me? Nothing!" The other people sitting on the bench clear out. I sit down and gesture for Poppy to do the same. She chooses to loom over me instead. My mother said not to tell Poppy what was going on because she might flip out, but I have to take my chances. "This is going to sound crazy," I say, "but I think Owen Elliott has been kidnapped by the men in black jackets who are trying to steal the plans for Blackout."

This is not what she expects me to say. It takes her an extra second to process my words. "*My* Blackout?" she asks. *Yes. Unless Owen Elliott has his* own *Blackout?* "Is *nothing* beneath you, Abby Hunter? What kind of trick are you trying to play to mess us up?"

This is taking too long. I need to know if she has any means to track Owen Elliott, and I need to know now.

"Listen up, Poppy," I say sternly, in my best Teflon voice. "There's a secret spy training facility under the Smith School. They are part of the Center. The Center helps protect our country from bad guys, and they've been chasing one called the Ghost for years. Are you keeping up? Confused? The Ghost wants Blackout because it can help him take over the world, which is his ultimate goal. He took your friend. He probably thinks Owen Elliott can give him the goods on Blackout. But he took *my* friends too. Now can you please stop being *so* difficult and just tell me if you can help?"

I expect a flicker of recognition. If Mrs. Smith is fast-tracking Poppy into the spy universe, surely Poppy has an inkling about the school. The slow realization that she does not hurts my insides. She's not even *trying* to get in.

"Spy school?" she says indignantly. "Ghosts? Do you think I'm some kind of idiot?"

"Think about it," I say. "Haven't you always known there is something strange about Smith?"

At this, she sits down, hard. Her shoulders sag. "What is going *on*? Blackout is just to make the girls next door *shut up*. They play music, they talk, they laugh *all* the time. I ask them to be quiet, but they ignore me, like they just can't be bothered. Blackout's just an experiment, you know, to see if I *could*. I swear, Abby, I will ruin your life if this is some ploy to beat us at the Challenge."

"I don't care about the Challenge," I say flatly.

"You don't?" She doesn't even try to hide her surprise.

"No. We can come in last place, and it doesn't matter."

"No way."

"Yup."

"Really truly?" she asks.

Every second I waste with Poppy puts me another second behind the men in black jackets. I'm about to practice my Crow on Poppy just to get things moving.

"Yes," I hiss. "What matters is our friends are *gone*."

Poppy thinks some more, eyes fixed upward on the giant blue whale, the gears turning in her head. "Tell me about the spy school," she says finally.

I've never had to explain the spy school to an outsider. Where do I start? I love Dorothy in *The Wizard of Oz*. She has a knack for trouble that I respect, and *she* started at the beginning, placing her red slipper on that first yellow brick. Seems a good idea.

"It began in the 1980s," I say. "They picked a bunch of girls to see how it would work. My mom, Jennifer Hunter, was one of them. And Mrs. Smith. You know, the headmaster." Poppy's expression changes from dubious to shocked. "Anyway, it's been going on ever since. The spy school trains the girls, and the Center sends them out on world-saving missions."

"And *you're* one of them?" she asks. *Oh, how I regret this already!*

"Not exactly."

"Well, what are you, then?"

"I'll have to get back to you on that," I say. "Did Owen Elliott have a phone on him? Something we can track? We need to find them, like, yesterday."

"Wait. Not so fast. I have *questions*."

I'm trying to be reasonable; after all, I need her. But her inability to see the urgency of this situation might make my head explode. Working with people not of your choosing is *hard*. "And I'll answer them," I say. "But first, can you locate the rest of Team OP or what?"

"Do you really call us that?" she asks.

"Yes. It has a nice ring to it, don't you think?"

She grimaces. "If this Ghosty person is going to end the world, why don't you just tell Mrs. Smith or your mother?"

"Long story." Mrs. Smith cannot not be trusted to make a mess of things, and Jennifer is *late*.

Poppy sits back and studies me. I am *not* telling her about the pirates, no matter how hard she stares. "Owen Elliott didn't show up on the GPS when I tried to find him before," she says after a pause. "His phone must be off."

My shoulders sag with disappointment. Spies make their own luck, but just once I'd like for something to break my way.

"However," says Poppy with a sly smile. "I sewed a piece of smart fabric into Owen's T-shirt to test it out. And I believe he is wearing that same T-shirt. I might be able to find him if I mess with the app code."

"Does he know?" I ask.

"Does it matter?" she shoots back. "I want to help him be his best self, and the fabric can make that happen. To be my friend, he has to make some changes."

I cannot believe I'm hearing this. Poppy is trying to mold Owen Elliott like a piece of clay. But now is not the time to explain why this is gross.

"You can change the app?" I ask.

"Of course," she says, indignant. Poppy pulls out her smartphone. "The fabric is not a tracker exactly, but with a few tweaks here and a couple of adjustments, it might work." As her fingers fly, she launches into a simultaneous lecture on how the smart fabric provides enhanced data to the user, enabling a person to be smarter about his or her own body. I nod enthusiastically while tuning her out. I just want to know if we can find Owen Elliott.

The crowds swell and churn around us. Our bench gets crowded. When Toby is concentrating on coding, he doesn't talk. Poppy is the opposite. She tells me about how she once had tea with the Queen of England.

"She has a lot of dogs," Poppy says. "They are every-where. I think she prefers them to people, which I totally get. I mean, people are unpredictable, right? They just do stupid *stuff*. Take Tucker Harrington III, for instance."

Finally! Something we can agree on. She transitions smoothly into a rant about Tucker and his penchant for disposable water bottles, fingers never leaving the small smartphone screen. I watch the people. There are no more men in black jackets, which means they believe they got what they need.

I want that to feel like a mistake.

Chapter 25

AN ICY WIND BLOWS IN.

WE SIT ON THE SQUISHED BENCH and wait for the updated app to acquire Owen Elliott's high-tech T-shirt. When I suggest we go outside for a better signal, Poppy scoffs. "I'm not deterred by stone walls," she says.

I know Charlotte and Izumi well enough that I can predict how they will likely react to things. But Poppy is confusing. She doesn't seem to experience the least bit of anxiety about Owen Elliott's safety. She peppers me with questions about the Center and spy school. I'm careful not to mention she's on the short list for entry, as she will then become insufferable and I will have to leave, despite her being my best and only hope for finding my friends.

"Got him," Poppy says finally, triumphantly. I grab for the phone, but she holds it beyond my reach. "Weird. They're moving . . . really fast. Look."

The screen contains a rudimentary map, nothing as fancy as the maps we've grown accustomed to. I expect to see them headed somewhere in the city, a secret Ghost lair, but the purple dot representing Owen Elliott zips along with no heed of roads or landscape. As if Owen Elliott is flying. Oh, no. This is not a good development.

"They're on a *plane*," I say.

Poppy's eyes go wide. "Flying? Where?"

I take the phone, this time without protest, and study the map. "West," I say.

"Do we chase after them? What do we do now? I do *not* understand the parameters of this problem. I need *data* so I can *plan*." Poppy is panicking. Her eyes pinwheel in her head, and her shoulders slide up toward her ears.

"I think I know how to figure this out," I say. It's a long shot, but I'm willing to give it a try. "You're good with computers, right?"

Poppy snorts. "Good? I'm great."

"I hope so," I say. "Come on."

We head back to the research library. "What do we need

a computer for?" asks Poppy, trailing behind me. "You have your phone. It's nice, by the way."

If only she knew. "We're going to contact a friend of mine," I say. Kind-of friend? Sort-of friend? "Iceman requires we make initial contact anonymously, through a public computer."

Poppy pulls up short. "Iceman? *The* Iceman? As in the *hacker*?" I nod. Poppy bursts out laughing. "No *way* you know Iceman. No. Way."

I shrug. "Sure I do."

"Prove it."

"That's what I'm *trying* to do." But sweat blooms on my forehead, and it's not from the heat. There's a good chance Iceman ignores my pleas, and that kind of humiliation will be catnip to Poppy.

Purple sits behind her research library desk, smacking her gum, staring at her phone.

"Ahem," I say. "Excuse me?"

She glances from me to Poppy. "You're back," she says. She does not sound happy about that. Before Poppy can open her big mouth and wreck this chance, I shove her behind me.

"Hi," I say brightly. "We're here at the museum working on a school project about evolution and early man. Everyone knows you have the premier proprietary collection on the subject, and we'd very much like to take a look at it."

"We sure do," Purple says, running her fingers through her hair. It barely moves. "However, you can only access it with an appointment."

Not good. What would Charlotte do? How would she convince this woman to let us in? Every second that passes my friends are further out of reach. My eyes drift to the plaques to the left of the door, engraved with the names of donors who helped finance this library. I go for the one in big letters on the very top.

"I hate to bring this up," I say casually, "but Elfreda Kurtz is my *grandmother*." I nod at the plaque, feeling Poppy's eyes burn into me. Purple glances up at the name. She mostly doesn't believe me, but there is a flicker of doubt.

"Where does she live?" Purple shoots back.

"Palm Springs," I blurt. "But she used to live here until the weather became too much for her. She made her fortune in shoes. And, um, shoelaces." Where is this coming from? Purple narrows her gaze. She's considering her answer carefully.

"How much trouble can two kids cause?" she mutters.

"None," I say quickly.

"That was a rhetorical question," she says. "Twenty minutes. Don't break anything."

We're in! Poppy's impressed. It's not like she says so, but I can tell. We choose a workstation out of Purple's line of sight, and I walk Poppy through the one hundred steps required to contact Iceman. By number twenty, she's convinced I'm lying. When the secret communication interface finally pops up, her jaw drops. "For real. How do *you* know Iceman?"

"It's a long story," I say.

"Another long story?"

"I'll tell you later." Or never. I instruct Poppy to include the gold spy phone number and the subject heading *Versailles*, the French palace where we first met Iceman last year. That should get her attention. Or I hope it does. We check the smart fabric app again. Owen Elliott is over the middle of the country now, barreling west at five hundred miles per hour. *Come on, Iceman. Don't let me down.*

We say good-bye to Purple, who tells me to say hello to Elfreda. With nothing to do but wait for Iceman, we stroll around the museum, half-heartedly checking out the exhibits. Poppy asks me about ten times to explain the Iceman connection and gets aggravated when I refuse. At one point she storms off, leaving me alone in the Hall of Minerals. I catch up to her in the Hall of Gems. She stares blankly into a case of multicolored quartz.

"We're going to lose the Challenge," she says glumly. "*I* never lose. This might be the first time."

I lose all the time. I could give her some tips. I stand silently by as she absorbs her new reality. When she woke up this morning, she was on one path, and now she's on another, stranded with me. I'm just about to launch into a pep talk on how to stay strong in the face of adversity and all that nonsense when my phone crackles and groans like it's being killed.

Everyone in the Hall of Gems turns in my direction.

"Malfunction," I say meekly, grabbing Poppy by the arm and dragging her past the meteorites and into the Spitzer Hall of Human Origins, which is empty because apparently no one cares about human origins today.

Huddled in a corner, I pull out the phone. An androgynous cartoon avatar with long hair in a rainbow of colors rides on a pink unicorn with a sparkling crystal horn. Pink. Iceman's favorite color. Yes! I almost fumble the phone trying to connect. Can excitement and terror exist side by side?

Iceman wastes no time with formalities. "What do you

want?" she asks, voice-altering software turning her into an evil robot.

"I need your help," I say bluntly.

"That's the way all my conversations begin," she says. But she doesn't disconnect, which I take as a good sign.

"It's about a plane," I say.

Chapter 26

THE ICEMAN EXPRESS.

POPPY HOPS AROUND behind me trying for a better view. "Is that him? What's with the unicorn? Will he help? What are we asking for anyway?"

"There's nothing to see," I bark. "It's a phone call!" Poppy's face collapses into a pout.

"Who are you talking to?" demands Iceman.

"No one. Poppy. Forget about her."

"You say there is a situation with a plane?" Iceman asks, already bored of me from the sound of it.

"Charlotte and Izumi and some other friends have been . . . well, kidnapped, and they're on a plane heading west and I need to know where they are going and then I need to go there. Does that make sense?"

"Abby," the robot voice echoes. "Your friends are always disappearing. You are bad luck." Bad luck. Something about those two little words slices to the heart of everything. I'm not careful enough. We never should have split up in the museum. My head swirls. "Abby? Are you still there? You know my price. Fifty thousand euros deposited into a Swiss numbered bank account."

"What?" Poppy barks, breaking out of her sulk. "That's crazy!"

"I don't have euros," I say. "Or dollars."

"That sounds familiar," Iceman says with a snicker. "What *do* you have?"

The last time we bargained for her services, I offered her glory, which was cheap and available. This time I barter Toby's Cookie app. She gets very quiet when I describe it. Of course, I leave out the bit about how it poisoned him. And how it doesn't work.

"I need to meet this Toby person one of these days," she says finally. "He sounds infinitely more interesting than you are. I will accept your offer."

I pump a fist skyward. Progress! "When will we hear back from you?" I ask.

"You caught me at a good time," she says. "It's a slow

day. Although the Argentinian government keeps calling. They're super needy. Making them wait might be a good lesson in patience."

I give her all the information I have, and Poppy explains how the smart fabric is tracking Owen Elliott. When Iceman is unimpressed by the smart fabric, Poppy returns to pouting. I miss my team. They don't pout.

"Give me ten minutes," Iceman says and abruptly hangs up.

"*Ten* minutes?" asks Poppy indignantly. "To hack air traffic control?"

"This is Iceman we're talking about," I remind her.

"Still," she huffs. I can almost see the wheels turning in her head. How does she one-up a person such as Iceman? Rather than tell her to forget it, I leave her to stew because that way I don't have to talk to her. I wander around the hall, stopping to admire Lucy, one of our early hominid ancestors, who looks pretty good for being four million years old. There's the life-size Neanderthals exhibit. They remind me of Tucker Harrington III, although that's insulting to the Neanderthals.

When Iceman calls back, her avatar has changed to a skeleton that looks a great deal like Lucy, except she has rainbow hair. Is this her way of telling me that I can't hide even if I want to? Creepiness aside, I'm glad she didn't just abandon me for the Argentinian government, and I dearly hope Toby doesn't kill me for trading his malfunctioning Cookie app for help.

"Your plane is en route to the Big Island," she says. The electronic voice has changed too—less robot, more artificial intelligence, like the GPS lady. "That's in Hawaii."

"I know that," I say. "*Why* are they going to the Big Island?"

"That is not a question I can answer, nor do I have much interest in it." Iceman has many abilities, but empathy is not among them. "Before you get all strung out," she continues, "I booked you and your Poppy on a flight out of JFK airport leaving in one hour." My phone *pings*. "And there are your tickets. You're cleared straight through, so you will be fine traveling as unaccompanied minors."

Poppy's jaw hangs open. I act like this is no big deal.

"You're the best, Ice," I say.

"I know that," she says. "And don't call me Ice."

"Got it."

"I will expect payment when your mission is complete."

She makes it sound so tidy and organized when in reality it is a giant mess. Once again, I am flying by the seat of my pants, hoping for the best. But this is not something to share with Iceman.

"Absolutely," I say. "I won't forget."

She hangs up without so much as an au revoir. I pull up the tickets. They look legit, and they include Poppy's full name. I cannot even begin to guess how she did this. Poppy can't either. She's freaking out as we hustle to the museum exit. An hour from Manhattan to JFK will require a miracle, but Poppy is more concerned that we're running away to Hawaii without telling anyone.

"Sometimes you have to break the rules," I explain. I don't mention that the last time I broke the rules, I ended up spending August deadheading rosebushes.

"I don't *know*," Poppy says. I dig a granola bar out of my backpack and hand it to her. Calories often make a bleak situation manageable. And we're going to Hawaii! Sure, it's not a vacation, and we won't get any beach time, but it's better than rainy old London or freezing-cold Paris. But this might just be me looking on the bright side.

"You don't have to come," I say. "You can head back to Briar and tell them you lost track of Owen Elliott. Play dumb."

"What I really want to do," she says, her accent crisp, "is go home and pretend I never heard of Smith or any of you. I didn't *want* to come to the United States in the first place! I was happy at my old school. I was happy in my old life! But no. My parents are never satisfied. It's always push, push, push. *Do more, Poppy. Be better, Poppy.*"

"You could do that, too," I say. "Go home, I mean." Although I'm not keen on calling Iceman back and asking her to rebook Poppy to London rather than Hawaii.

"Oh, forget that," she says. "Quitting equals failure in their book. And they *never* let me forget a failure. When I was in third grade, I didn't get the lead in the class play, and they still talk about it. I was *eight*."

Standing before me on a sidewalk rippling with heat, with the clock ticking, I suddenly understand her friendship with Owen Elliott. They both see everything in life, good and bad, through a lens of parental judgment. They are motivated by pressure from the outside, not by what they feel on the inside.

And how am I any different, trying my hardest to prove to Mrs. Smith that I'm worthy of spy school? Do I even remember why I want it so badly? But the minute Izumi, Charlotte, and Toby disappeared, everything changed. This is no longer about proving myself or saving the world. It's about saving my friends. That is the *only* thing that matters. I watch as Poppy struggles with the pros and cons of coming or going. The push and pull plays out on her face. Finally, she gives me a half smile, half grimace.

"I owe Owen Elliott," she says. "He's the only one at school who's nice to me. I'm coming."

"Are you sure?" I ask. "Because once you're in, you're *in*. It's not like you can change your mind later."

She waves me off. "I know! Quit lecturing me. We only have an hour. Why are we wasting time?"

Seriously. I don't like this temporary partnership. It's hard work.

We leap in a cab and every time it slows down, my heartbeat speeds up. What happened to New York City cabbies driving like complete maniacs? Doesn't this guy know the fate of the world might be at stake? We pull to the curb with twenty-five minutes until departure. There is no way. In the best of times, this airport is a crush of confused people all moving in different directions, speaking seven hundred different languages. We throw some elbows to get to the security line and look sad and pathetic to *cut* the security line. Charlotte would be proud.

As promised, no one raises an eyebrow as we make our way through the various checkpoints to our gate. No one asks how come we're alone or who is picking us up on the other side. Iceman's magic makes them believe all is okay, even if appearances suggest otherwise.

The first-class seats are a nice touch. I wonder how much more it adds to my debt. She must think the Cookie app is cooler than it is. It doesn't even *work*! Poppy wraps herself in a thin blue blanket and immediately demands two glasses of cranberry juice from the flight attendant. We check the smart fabric tracker one last time before stowing our small backpacks under the seats in front of us. Charlotte, Izumi, Toby, and Owen Elliott are about two and a half hours ahead of us. Do they even know where they are going? Are they scared?

I stare out the window as the world flies by below. Poppy nudges me. "I never attacked you down at the docks," she says. "Just so you know. I have no idea what you meant."

And the truth is, I believe her. That flash of blue and yellow in the locker room, just out of the corner of my eye, that was Jane Ann's butterfly boys watching me copy Poppy's idea book. They thought getting my phone could solve all their problems. They didn't count on it being the wrong phone. Or me smashing it to bits.

I take advantage of the downtime to rehearse the speech I will give Toby to explain why I bartered away the Cookie app. But no matter how I present it, I just don't see him being all that excited by the idea.

Chapter 27

A LOVELY, TROPICAL, EVIL LAIR.

THE BIG ISLAND IS FAR. Come on, Ghost! Why not a New York evil lair, preferably one within walking distance of the museum? But that would be simple, and simple and I have never met. I watch three movies and ask for multiple rounds of warm chocolate chip cookies because the flight attendant seems to have an endless supply.

Finally, the pilot announces that we are beginning our descent. I check the tracker. Owen Elliott's T-shirt appears to be at an old coffee plantation on the southeastern side of the island, very close to the Pacific Ocean.

I've been a lot of places—weird places—but I've never been to Hawaii. I guess Jennifer never had any contacts here. I nudge Poppy and show her the tracker. "We should be able to get a bus," I say.

"Why not Uber?"

"Because Uber is not anonymous."

She raises her eyebrows. "You think they think we're coming after them? Us? Enough to check Uber records?"

"They might," I respond.

"No bus," she says.

"Have you ever even been on a bus?" I ask.

"I live in *London*," she shoots back. As if that answers my question. Poppy seems like the chauffeur-driven type.

"And?"

She flushes red. "No."

I snicker. "It's fun. You'll *love* it." Another reason why Poppy will make an awful spy. She's never ridden on a bus! So why does Mrs. Smith want her so badly?

We arrive in the late afternoon, having traveled back in time six hours, tripping lightly across five time zones. As we have no luggage other than our small backpacks, we are out at the curb in record time. The air smells sweet, like tropical flowers and pineapple. Thinking about Toby and his Cookie app, I wonder if they pump in the smell so when visitors encounter fragrant flowers or pineapple in regular life, their memory brings them right back to lovely Hawaii. It's a nice idea. I see why it appealed to him.

The tropical flowers are not having the intended effect on Poppy, however. She grumbles about the poor working conditions of being a spy on the run, as in buses and no built-in beach time. I ignore her. The bus is late. Island time. I try to go with it, but my eyebrow twitches. I try my mother, but she still doesn't answer. I hope she knows we're not at Briar anymore.

Twenty minutes later, when I'm almost ready to start walking, the bus pulls into the stop. People with suitcases get off, and people with suitcases get on. I check the route map inside the bus to make sure we're going in the right direction. The stop will get us close, but I suspect there will be trekking through some dense Hawaiian jungle. If we're lucky, there will be plants with thorns and maybe ants or biting spiders. Big ones.

I wonder how Poppy will like that?

Chapter 28

NOW I GET IT.

OF COURSE, IT STARTS TO RAIN the minute we step off the bus. This happens in the tropics. Thick gray clouds move swiftly across the sky, position themselves directly above us, and dump buckets. Water drips off the brim of my Smith School baseball hat. On the bright side, our luggage doesn't get wet because we don't have any.

The bus driver asked several times if we were sure we wanted to get off at this stop. This is probably because there is nothing here but plant life. He was right to be concerned.

"Where are we?" Poppy demands, rain flattening her red hair.

"The plantation is that way," I say pointing in a vague direction because I'm not entirely sure where the plantation is. Since about five miles back, Owen Elliott's tracker went wonky. We might be in a dead zone, or maybe it's natural interference.

Caused by a giant thunderstorm, for instance.

Lightning zigzags to the ground, followed by a loud *crack*. The air hums with electricity. Poppy literally jumps into my arms. We tumble over into the mud.

"Thunder!" she howls, burying her head in my shoulder. Water seeps through my shorts and fills my sneakers.

"Get off me!"

"I hate thunder!" Curling up in a tight ball, she presses her palms to her ears and squeezes her eyes shut. She's not kidding she hates thunder. I half cajole, half drag her to the shoulder to avoid death by passing vehicle. She remains in her defensive hedgehog position in the middle of a dirty puddle.

In five minutes, the storm blows over. The air is scrubbed clean. I poke Poppy in the shoulder. "Hey. You can come out now. It's over."

"Are you sure?" she asks, unmoving in her puddle.

"Pretty sure."

"You need to be totally sure."

"The sky is blue!" I yell. One eyeball peeks out from behind her hand to verify I'm telling the truth.

"That was my worst nightmare," she says, shaking loose her arms and legs.

Boy, I'd love it if my worst nightmare were a little rain. My current worst nightmare is the Ghost achieving world domination. "Come on," I say. "We don't have a lot of time."

Before she can move, Poppy has to spend a full minute being horrified by the mud covering her head to toe. But being a spy involves discomfort, and it's better to know that up front.

On the edge of the old coffee fields, I scan the horizon. There is nothing to see, but somewhere out there is Owen Elliott's last known location, so that is where we are going. I trudge forward into the overgrown fields. Eventually, Poppy follows, grumbling.

We hike over uneven ground, full of holes obscured by waist-high grasses with razor-sharp edges. Each step is a chore. Overhead, birds chatter enthusiastically. I don't speak bird, but I sure hope they are not warning us away.

Poppy drags behind. "This is my second-worst nightmare," she mutters. "Nature. Yuck." Ignoring her, I do a mental inventory of my gear. Protective baseball hat, check. Spy phone, check. Exploding candy, check. Rainbow shoelaces, check. Now if I only had some idea what was waiting for us up ahead, I'd be in good shape.

"How much longer?" Poppy asks every two minutes. My refusal to answer does nothing to diminish her enthusiasm for the question. But she's right. This is taking a long time. I might be leading us in circles.

Just when Poppy is close to mutiny, the peaked roof of a grand white mansion comes into view. My first thought is relief quickly followed by dismay. This is the very definition of isolation, and we have no way to contact the outside world if things go awry. Iceman has surely wiped clean our flight details by now. If we disappear, no one will even know where to start looking. I keep this doomsday scenario to myself.

We move a little closer, squatting in the brush at the perimeter of mowed grass and fancy landscaping for a better look. The house, with white clapboard siding and a wraparound porch, sprawls in every direction. There are three visible outbuildings, a barn, a garage, and a guesthouse. This means our people could be in one of four places. I shiver, despite the warm, humid air.

"Here's the plan," I whisper. "We get into the house. Find everyone. Leave."

Poppy snaps out of her nature-induced funk long

enough to look incredulous. "*That's* your plan?"

"Do you have a better one?" I demand.

"Undoubtedly," she says. "This is basically a search and rescue. First, we deal with the dogs. There are three of them. See? Guard dogs. They should respond to hand signals, which I happen to know because my father shows standard poodles in the Westminster Kennel Club Dog Show every year, and the commands are generally the same. Once the dogs are down, we move on to the guards. There are also three of them, but you probably already saw that. One is sleeping. They must be on a rotation, so all we do is wait one or two cycles and figure out the best time for us to move undetected. I suggest we start with the main building and systematically work our way back in this direction. Once we know the guards' rotation, that should be easy. At this time of day, the buildings will provide ample shadow for us to remain hidden if we stay on the west side. If there is a building we can't access, we navigate the perimeter and look for a weakness. An open window, an unlocked door. Once we gain access, we reconnoiter. Basements are good for hiding hostages as are attics. Questions to consider: How many people are inside the various buildings? Do they have information? Can we neutralize them? I don't see any signs of occupancy from here, but that may change when we get closer. We don't want to get in a situation where they send out an intruder alarm or anything. Oh, and we do all this quietly. Naturally."

She stops for a breath. My heart constricts. I didn't even notice the dogs. Or the sleeping guard. I was too busy thinking about Izumi and Charlotte and Toby locked up in one of these benign-looking buildings, hungry, thirsty, scared.

Suddenly, I understand exactly why Poppy will be accepted into the spy school and I will not.

Chapter 29

GOING TO THE DOGS.

POPPY CONTINUES TO EXPLAIN how we will evacuate the hostages if, in fact, we find them, and how we will proceed if we don't. Her plan has contingencies and fallbacks and fail-safes. It has an emergency escape route. It rolls off her tongue as if by magic, rife with important details I would not have picked up if I'd stood here and assessed the situation for a century.

A good spy must accept her limitations and carry on regardless. But *am* I a good spy? Or am I just reckless? Poppy eyes me, waiting patiently for feedback. She is not interested in my self-doubt. And it certainly won't save anyone's life. I shake it off. I can doubt myself later.

"That's a great plan," I say quietly.

Hunkered down uncomfortably in the tall grass, we observe the guards until Poppy is sure of their rotation schedule. "Every fifteen minutes, they move one position clockwise." The dogs, however, follow no such routine. They roam freely, snuffling at the ground, on the lookout for trespassers. They are big, burly dogs with square heads and jaws full of sharp teeth. I surely hope Poppy's Westminster Kennel Club poodle commands work or this will be one short rescue.

On Poppy's insistence we approach from the west, shrouded in long shadows. The first dog to spot us creeping along is black and brown. He growls, bits of slobber dangling from his lips. My mouth goes dry. Beside me, Poppy starts winging her arms all over the place like she's a baby bird about to take flight. There is no way this works. We are dog food.

But just like that, the dog whines, lies on the ground, and covers his stubby snout with his paws. Poppy gives him a vigorous rub between the ears, and the dog actually sighs with pleasure. We leave him begging for belly rubs as we dash across an open stretch of grass between the buildings.

The next two dogs go down equally fast. I'll admit, I'm a little dazzled.

"Now." Poppy gives me a shove. The guards are rotating, the dogs are down, and it's time to go for the big house. And if we run smack into ten armed guards inside, I bet Poppy has a plan for what to do about that, too.

But there is no one inside the house's entryway, a good sign. We bolt into the nearest room and throw ourselves behind a couch upholstered in fabric like a Hawaiian shirt gone bad. Pineapples and orchids, I think. Panting, I adjust my baseball hat. I'm shocked we are actually in the house and not chewed up on the lawn. Poppy's cheeks burn red with adrenaline. Her hands shake. We wait another few minutes. No one appears. All is quiet.

"The kitchen is that way," Poppy whispers. "I noticed an air vent on the roof toward the back of the house. Probably a stove exhaust. Typically, the cellar would be off the kitchen and used for cold storage. That's where we look first."

She's killing me. Stove exhaust? Cold storage? We sneak to the kitchen. True to her word, there is a basement door. I should be happy. I'm not.

The kitchen is empty too. Poppy looks longingly at the sink. "Do you think I have time to wash my hands?" she whispers.

"Forget it," I whisper back. The basement door is

jammed but yields to a good jarring kick. Poppy leaps out of her skin at the noise.

"I said quietly!" she hisses. I will never live it down if I blow our cover. But no one appears. This is because there is nothing interesting in the basement except baskets of onions and potatoes. There are two refrigerators and three chest-style freezers where, in the movies, they always hide the dead body. Fortunately, I discover only hunks of frozen meat.

"Nothing," I say, heading back to the stairs.

Off the kitchen, there is a set of back stairs to the second floor of the house. I'm halfway up when I realize Poppy is not behind me. She's still in the kitchen, a weird look on her face, pointing at a few bulging plastic trash bags lined up waiting for removal.

"Look," she whispers.

"What? Are they not sorting their recycling correctly?"

"*No.*" She stabs her finger at one of the bags where the bottom hem of a distinctly blue Smith T-shirt peeks out. Gingerly, I remove it from the bag. It's damp and stained. Poppy's eyes go as big as saucers.

"Is that . . . blood?" she asks.

When I put the T-shirt up close to my nose and take a sniff, she almost heaves. "Coke," I say. "And maybe soy sauce."

She grabs the shirt, roughly turning it inside out to reveal a bit of fabric stitched to the inside. The smart fabric. Owen's T-shirt.

"Well, at least I know why it stopped functioning," she says, shaking it at me. "I'm still working on *waterproofing*." She seems relieved that the smart fabric failed due to outside circumstances and not some deficit of hers when really, she should be concerned that Owen Elliott is not *in* the T-shirt. "And how could he be so casual with *my* intellectual property?"

My jaw hangs open. "Did it occur to you that maybe Owen Elliott didn't want to take off the T-shirt, but he was forced?"

"What? Oh. *Oh!* I didn't think of that."

"I'm sure he's fine," I say, as much to her as to myself. I poke at the remaining contents of the trash bag, but there are no other familiar items in among the plastic yogurt containers and empty cereal boxes. Poppy tucks the dirty T-shirt into her back pocket, where it dangles like a soft blue tail.

We head to the second floor of the house. Poppy is quiet as we poke our heads into each room, turning up exactly nothing. The top floor is more of the same, although the ocean view from up here is spectacular. Overall, views aside, the main house is a bust.

It's now mostly dark outside. A glow lingers from the sunset. Poppy informs me that we will search the barn, garage, and guesthouse counterclockwise to avoid the guards. I want to argue, to poke holes in her perfectly laid-out plan. But I can't find any.

We exit the main building through the kitchen back door, maybe a little too comfortable with how easily we've evaded detection thus far. That is always when trouble shows up. And right now, trouble is in the form of an angry dog with glistening black eyes. Poppy throws out a few hand signals to quiet him, but he doesn't respond. Instead, he sinks low and growls.

"He must have failed school," she whispers as the dog moves closer. He licks his lips, envisioning how good we will taste.

"What's the plan, Poppy?" I ask. Our backs are flat against the side of the house. If we run, the dog catches us and eats us. If we stay, the dog goes straight to eating us.

"I . . . I don't know . . . I . . . This should *work*. . . ."

It's not working. I have another idea, but Poppy is not going to like it. Moving very slowly so as not to further alarm our furry nemesis, I pull the spy phone from my backpack.

"Social media?" Poppy hisses. "Now?" I ignore her,

holding the phone up so it recognizes my face and grants me access. I secure the hat on my head. I'm going to buy us some time.

"Plug your ears," I say. The dog is so close I can smell his last meal.

"What?"

"Stick your fingers in your ears. Do it now." There is no way her fingers will be enough, but I only have one hat.

Poppy jams her pointer fingers in her ears. "Whatever you are going to do, do it now."

I tap the blaring horn app. The phone grows scalding hot in my hand, and I can barely hold on to it. The dog's ears perk up, his head pivoting rapidly from side to side. He whines as his tail tucks between his legs. And then he pitches forward on his face.

Unfortunately, Poppy also pitches forward on her face. I tuck the scorching phone gingerly into my shorts, grab her by the arms, and drag her awkwardly around the dog and across the lawn to the barn. She makes weird little noises every time I hit a rock or a bump, and after about thirty seconds she says something that sounds like *I'm going to kill you, Abby*.

But I can't be sure.

Chapter 30

NO ONE HERE BUT THE BAD GUYS.

KEEPING ONE EYE on the dog, who doesn't even twitch, I drag Poppy through the barn door. Inside are ten abandoned horse stalls. Rusted farm tools lean against a weather-worn wall. By the time I drag Poppy through a few piles of hay and something else that I can't identify but doesn't smell great, she's mostly awake. I think I liked her better the other way.

"What did you do to me?" she yells. "How *dare* you?"

"Be quiet!" I yell back. "I didn't have a choice." But did I? Could I have used the bees instead? *Don't second-guess yourself, Abby. You did what you had to. Sometimes there is collateral damage in spying.*

Poppy staggers to her feet, bent over, hands on knees, and for a second I'm concerned she might puke. Toby did not mention side effects, but usually the apps are reserved for bad guys, so if they feel a little lousy afterward, well, too bad.

"*What* was that?" Poppy demands, holding her head in her hands.

"What?" I ask innocently.

"You knocked out the dog," she replies. "And *me*."

"Oh. That. Right. Well, let's see. Toby might have given us a few toys before we left Briar."

"That was no toy."

"I mean spy gear. Gadgets. Things to help you buy time. When you need it. To escape. Like we just did."

Poppy drops her head back to her knees. "I cannot believe this is my life," she says. "I was supposed to win the Challenge. Get the glory. Instead, I'm stuck out here with you."

"I could leave you here, if you want."

"Shut up," she hisses. "And tell me what other tricks you have up your sleeve. Maybe if you'd *shared* them, I'd have come up with a better plan."

I'm about to lob back a snarky reply when I realize she's right. For all intents and purposes, at this moment,

Poppy and I are *a team*. And I withheld vital information. If Veronica knew, she'd be so disappointed.

I open the spy phone and show her the defensive apps: the horn, with which she is now familiar, the bees, the snarling dog, and the lightning bolt. I try not to get too anxious over how the horn drained my battery.

"What's with the cookies?" she asked. "That's what you traded to Iceman, right? What does it do?"

For the first time, I notice the Cookie app is not blurred out on this phone. "No," I say quickly, not wanting to explain that I was less than honest with Iceman. "That was something else. The cookies are nothing. And by the way, I also have exploding candy and shoelaces." Poppy's jaw goes a little slack.

"Are you kidding me with all this?" she asks.

"Not at all," I answer.

"Wow," she says, picking a bit of hay out of her hair. "Toby should win the Challenge. I mean, look at this stuff."

"Don't forget the bad guys want *your* technology, so that makes you kind of the default best, even if it's in a really bad way."

She puzzles over my logic and dismisses it with a shrug. "I guess, but still, this stuff is cool." Now would be a good time to tell her that, provided we survive, she will soon be recruited to join the spy school, and the gear will be infinitely cooler than deafening horns. But I can't bring myself to do it. There will be time later.

"There's nothing here," I say instead. "We should move on to the garage."

The garage is like an airplane hangar, with a concrete floor, a high roof, and bright lights. Dozens of exotic cars sit silently in two lines, gleaming and beautiful. We creep along, peeking into each vehicle just in case. Poppy stops at a red convertible two-seater that is about five inches off the ground. It looks terribly uncomfortable to sit in.

"A Ferrari Spider, probably 1957," she says thoughtfully. "It's worth about thirty-five million dollars. Mint condition."

"What?" I bleat. Who would spend that much money on a car that doesn't even get driven from the looks of it? Poppy runs her hand lovingly over the glossy finish.

"I like cars," she says. "Especially old ones. They make perfect sense to me. Everything has a purpose."

We continue our search, but there is no sign of Charlotte, Izumi, Toby, or Owen Elliott. I'm about to express my doubts about this whole venture when Poppy yelps and drops to the concrete floor between a silver roadster and another Ferrari, which are a dime a dozen in this swanky garage. I hit the ground next to her. It's a man in a cowboy hat and flip-flops, with a bulky satellite phone mushed against the side of his head. He paces up one row of cars and down the other, dragging his fingers along the fancy vehicles absentmindedly. Suddenly, he is right next to us. I could reach out and touch his foot. Gross. The last thing I will remember will be a toenail green with fungus. But he's on the phone, completely oblivious to our presence.

"We're close," he says, eyes unfocused. "The kids have the information—they *must*. They just need to be properly *motivated* to share it, and that happens to be my specialty. It'll get done. I have ideas. I'm heading down there in a few minutes to get started."

His eyes drift right over us. *Right* over us. And yet he sees nothing. I guess this is why you're not supposed to drive and talk on a cell phone at the same time. I squeeze my eyes shut and try not to breathe. Done with his phone call, the man gives the pretty Ferrari a kiss on its hood and finally leaves. His heavy footsteps disappear out of the garage.

"That was close," Poppy says, her face shiny with sweat. "Too close."

"He said 'down there.' Did you hear that?"

She nods. "We checked the cellar in the main house, remember? Nada."

I peer through a window as the man vanishes into the murky night. The casual way he discussed getting them to talk has turned my stomach.

"No matter what, we need to hurry up, find them, and get out of here."

"You make it sound like no big deal," says Poppy, "when really it is."

If our lives weren't in imminent danger, I'd explain to her that it's better if I don't consider the big picture, as in stopping the world's most notorious criminal from bringing down modern civilization, because with stakes that high, I wouldn't even get out of bed. Instead, I break everything into chunks, small pieces, micro steps. That way it feels like no big deal.

I'm sure the guesthouse will have a "down there," but it's a completely empty, single-story building. There aren't even any dust bunnies. We sit on the floor of the main room, on either side of the window, out of sight.

"I need to think," Poppy says, pressing her palms into her eye sockets.

"We know they're here," I say. "We *missed* something."

"Yes," she agrees. "The place where they are being held."

I stretch my legs out in front of me and lean into the wall. Tropical air floats in through the window. It's not fair that the bad guys get to hang out in such a nice place. Evil lairs should not be on tropical islands. It's just wrong.

"I wish I were back at Smith," Poppy says glumly.

"Wait a minute. Did you just wish you were back at *school*?"

She nods. "School is like the old cars. It's orderly. I know what's expected, even if I don't enjoy it. Out here, this, it's just *chaos*. And I really don't like chaos."

Suddenly, I have an enormous, amazing thought. What if Mrs. Smith wants Poppy to be part of a *team*, like she was with Jennifer? In the 1980s, when my mother was a budding spy, Lola Smith was her best friend and handler. Lola did the planning. Jennifer did the running around trying not to get killed.

Yes! This makes *perfect* sense. Poppy *is* Mrs. Smith! She is probably being brought on to work with one of the older girls. I don't know why I was so hung up on the idea that it was Poppy *or* us. We still have a chance of getting into spy school, especially if we can bring the Center a Ghostly head on a platter.

Hugging Poppy is weird and inappropriate in light of our current circumstances, but I do it anyway. She goes stiff as a board. I guess she's not the hugging type.

"What was that for?" she asks.

"If things go badly," I say, "and they probably will, I want you to know I'm glad you're here with me." Poppy's lips flap in the breeze. Her cheeks flush. Her eyes water. "What's wrong?"

"Nothing," she stutters. "I just . . . well . . . never mind. Thanks for not leaving me behind in New York."

"You're welcome," I say. It's time to regroup, and we should do that somewhere beyond the reach of the dogs. "Let's sneak back toward the road. We can strategize about what to do next from there."

Poppy perks up at the mention of strategy. "I have ideas," she says.

That figures.

Chapter 31

CANDY IS BAD FOR YOU.

WE UNWIND OUR EFFORTS, moving past the garage, the barn, and the guesthouse, around the main house, across the lawn, and back toward the overgrown fields. All goes perfectly until there is a little yelp and Poppy vanishes. When I turn around, she's *gone*.

"Poppy! Where are you?"

"Down here." Her voice rises from near my feet. I flick on my phone flashlight to find I'm two inches from falling through a jagged fissure in the earth. Poppy, apparently, wasn't so lucky. "Get me out!"

Flat on my belly, I shine the light into the crack, the beam catching Poppy's panicked eyes about ten feet below me. She's tumbled into a cave, with smooth rock walls and damp ground. But maybe it's more of a tunnel because, shining the light in either direction, I can't see the ends. This also means there is no way for Poppy to climb back out.

"Weird," I say.

"Did you not hear the part where I asked you to get me out of here?" Anger has replaced fear.

"I don't think I can," I say.

"I am *not* staying down here alone!" she cries. "It's freezing!" I roll over on my back, to think without her staring up at me. There is no one we can ask for help. I don't have any rope, and I couldn't pull her out even if I did. This leaves one option.

"Watch out that I don't land on you," I say, throwing my legs over the ragged edge of the opening.

"You're coming down here?"

"Yeah. I think this is a lava tube system. We should be able to find a way out."

"Should?"

"Would you rather I just leave you there and go for help?"

"No!"

"I figured. Now move."

Poppy presses her back against the far side of the cave while I calculate the best way to fall ten feet without breaking anything. But Poppy did it, so I sure can. There is no way she's better at tumbling into mysterious holes in the ground than I am. I close my eyes and shove myself into the darkness, landing with an undignified *thud* that echoes off the rock.

Poppy suppresses a smirk but just barely. "Graceful," she says.

"I've been practicing," I respond, dusting off my shorts and checking to make sure I have not inadvertently shattered the gold spy phone. My relief that it is intact is completely out of proportion with our situation.

I shine the light in both directions. I'm right. It's a tunnel with a trickle of water running through it. And isn't underground a good place to hide something you don't want found?

Like the evil headquarters of the world's most notorious criminal?

"You may have literally fallen into something here," I say. Above my head, the smooth rock drips with moisture.

"We should go left," Poppy says.

"Why?"

"Why what?"

"Why left?" I ask.

"Because it's the correct way to go," she snaps.

"How do you know?"

Poppy puts her hands on her hips and glares. "Why do you think it's wrong?"

"I don't. Necessarily." The truth is I'm not sure why I'm arguing. Left is as good as right when you have no idea where you are going. I'm wasting time.

"Fine. You choose," she says.

I point my flashlight into the gloom. "Rock, paper, scissors," I say. "I win, we go right. You win, we go left."

"You're not even kidding, are you?"

"Nope."

"No wonder you are always in trouble. This is no way to make a decision."

I win. We go right. Poppy sulks. The water grows deeper, sloshing around my ankles as I plow forward. My teeth chatter so aggressively I might bite off my tongue. I did not think Hawaii would be so cold. Of course, underground Hawaii is not exactly the beach.

The lava tube bends and curves. We encounter a beautiful green pool where the water reaches our knees. By the time we crawl out on the other side, Poppy's lips are blue.

"This is like a labyrinth," Poppy says, shivering. "Did

you know that was where they held the first Minotaur hostage? Otherwise, he'd just go around eating all the people."

That is a lovely thought. Thank you, Poppy. I'm about to point this out to her when she grabs my arm. "Hold on," she whispers. In the distance is a flicker. An actual light at the end of the tunnel!

I click off my flashlight to conserve battery, and we proceed in total silence except for the splashing, which can't be helped. The lava tube grows wider and taller. The flicker grows steady and bright, finally revealing a large cavern ahead. Built into the cavern is a room that looks like the one from the NASA mission to the moon: rows of desks and computers, manned by grim-looking adults in layers of warm clothing—the Ghost's minions. He's probably tucked away in some fancy penthouse in Paris or Tokyo while these cold, gray people do his bidding. He's a bad guy who doesn't like to get his hands dirty, unlike Tinker Bell, who seemed to relish the idea of squeezing information from me.

Everything looks very new and shiny. There are even unpacked boxes. The Ghost must have relocated his headquarters here recently. Off to one side of the space, a ladder leads to an opening in the lava above. This must be the main entrance—much more civilized than the fissure

Poppy fell through. If I had to guess, I'd say the plantation is right above us, providing the perfect camouflage.
Beyond the room, the tube continues, bending out of
sight.

"I'm betting they are over *there* somewhere," Poppy
whispers, gesturing to the disappearing tunnel on the far
side. I agree. Which means all we have to do is get through
this cavern undetected by *all* the people. No problem.

"Those exploding candies," Poppy says. "You still have
them?" I nod. "Great. We create a diversion and make a run
for it."

Oh, I like that. Why didn't I think of it? I dump the
contents of my backpack on the ground, picking out a few
candies and the shoelaces. Mushed together, four caramels are roughly the size of a golf ball. I wrap the golf ball
in a three-inch length of shoelace. Taking careful aim, I
hurl the golf ball in a sweet arc over the workers to the
front of the cave, where it hits the rock wall and explodes
in a fury of light and smoke. The grim-looking adults drop
what they are doing and panic.

"Code red!"

"Fire extinguisher."

"Run!"

"Remain calm!"

"Do not abandon your posts!"

The caramels spit multicolored sparks and blue fire, plumes of smoke rising to the cavern roof. We sprint through the chaos for the other side, and no one comes close to noticing.

Chapter 32

BUY TIME. USE IT WISELY.

AT FIRST, I THINK POPPY is hysterical, but it turns out she is full-on giggling. "That was the *best*," she gasps, collapsing against the rock wall. "Let's blow something else up." This is not what I expected.

"No," I say sternly. "We only use the spy gear when we're desperate."

"Where is the fun in that?" she whines. If she can't figure that out, she is not as smart as everyone thinks. The little stream is deeper on this side. My legs are fully numbed to the knees. At some point, we are going to sustain permanent damage, and I will have a lot of explaining to do to Poppy's parents.

"Wouldn't hot chocolate be good right now?" I ask as we slog along. "With marshmallows."

"Warm apple pie," Poppy replies immediately. "Skip the ice cream, please."

"Mac and cheese. Still bubbling from the heat."

"Oh, I'd like to stick my feet in that!"

"How about a pot of chicken soup?"

"I'm not picky."

"Tea with honey."

"Hot apple cider."

Warmth flares in my stomach. I'm just about to add French fries, crisp and hot right out of the fryer, when the tunnel bends and I find myself face-to-face with Izumi. Her hair is wild and her T-shirt torn.

"Abby!"

"Izumi!"

"What are you doing here?"

"Rescuing you?"

She hugs me so hard and for so long that Poppy starts making impatient noises. "I am *so* glad to see you," Izumi says, ignoring Poppy.

"What happened? Where are the others?"

"They separated us," she says with a shudder. "And I

got sick of sitting around some stupid lava cell freezing to death, so I left."

"You just walked out of your cell?" asks Poppy.

Izumi glances at her. "Well, they hadn't gotten around to adding bars or anything. So yeah, I kind of just left."

"Should we be worried?" I ask, glancing over Izumi's shoulder.

"It's probably a few minutes before the guard regains consciousness," Izumi says casually. It's statements like these that make me realize how far off the normal curve we actually are.

"Did you just say what I think you said?" asks Poppy.

"Yeah," I say, grinning. "We better get moving."

"Wait!" Poppy steps between us. "Are there guards? Is there security? What exactly are we dealing with here?"

"She really likes to plan," I say to Izumi, with a shrug.

"Wow. That's different. Okay. There was the guard outside my cave and two farther down the lava tube. I figure that's where the others are being held."

Poppy processes this. She swipes my phone. "Here's what we do," she says. "We sneak up and take out the two guards with the bee thingy."

Izumi glances at me. "You *told* her?"

"I had no choice," I say defensively.

"Can you guys pay attention?" Poppy snaps. "Once we spring the others, we follow the water, which must flow out of the lava tubes at some point. That's how we escape."

"The bee will kill the phone charge," I say, in the spirit of full disclosure.

Poppy is unconcerned. "Do we have any exploding shoelace left? Yes? Good. We can use it as a diversion. If they start chasing us."

"Oh, they'll definitely chase us," says Izumi.

"They always do," I add.

Poppy eyes us. "I'm not sure if I hate hanging out with you guys or if it's the most fun I've ever had."

"The end tends to get messy," Izumi offers. "I'd reserve judgment until then."

"Any comments on the plan?" Poppy asks. "No? Good. Let's move out."

Spies do not "move out." We aren't soldiers. But we follow her anyway.

The tube narrows and shrinks. If I were any taller, I'd knock myself out. Poppy is just fine letting Izumi take the lead. We move slowly and cautiously, on the lookout for the random guards Izumi says float the tunnels. My left thumb rests just above the bee app. Ready as I'll ever be.

"How much farther?" I ask Izumi.

"It's just up here," she answers. "I think. These stupid tubes all look the same after a while."

"Hey!" A deep voice echoes off the walls. We stop short. Poppy, at the end of our parade, squeezes her eyes shut. "What are you kids doing down here?"

The guard is dressed in military-style fatigues, with a tight wool hat and heavy gloves. A rifle of some variety is slung over his chest, a walkie-talkie clipped to his jacket.

The gloves are thick enough that I calculate I have a split second before he can get a finger free to key the walkie-talkie. Or get to the gun. I aim the phone and tap the bee, hoping as hard as I can that I'm right.

The phone turns instantly hot, but I can't let go. I lunge for Owen's T-shirt, dangling from Poppy's back pocket, and wrap it around the phone as tiny sparkling glass beads blast out of the front. The guard throws up his hands, but it's too late. The swarm is upon him. He howls, flailing blindly as the glass beads continue to pelt him. It's all I can do to hold the phone steady, heat working through the layers of T-shirt to my flesh.

The guard hits the ground, arms wrapped protectively around his head. A single bee sting is painful enough. I can't imagine a swarm feels very good. But they aren't real bees, just glass copies, and he will recover soon enough.

"Go!" I shout. The trick to buying time is spending it wisely. We do a mad dash down the tube. Right now, our guard is pulling off his gloves and calling his buddies. He'll tell them he was attacked. He'll say kids are running amok in the tubes. He'll send a swarm of his own.

We have to hurry.

Chapter 33

HOW ABOUT A SWIM?

WE DUCK INTO the first cell to avoid the two guards rushing past, summoned to help their friend, surprisingly attacked by bees, and there is Charlotte, twirling a length of hair and grinning. "I knew you'd show up eventually," she says, jumping up and dusting off her shorts.

Toby, a little farther down the lava tube, does not seem surprised when we appear. "I heard screaming," he says. "I figured the chances you were somehow involved were fifty-fifty."

I'm feeling pretty positive about our rescue efforts until we find Owen Elliott, up against his wall, in fetal position, shivering. He wears a horrible bright blue–and-yellow

Hawaiian shirt. His eyes, half-closed, drift over us.

"You definitely don't want this guy on your team when the zombie apocalypse happens," Charlotte murmurs, appraising the situation.

"No self-respecting zombie would eat that shirt," Toby adds.

"Hey," Poppy says to Owen Elliott. "Get up. Come on. We're going."

Owen Elliott shakes his head and closes his eyes tightly, as if he can make us disappear. "I'm not going anywhere with you guys," he says. "Not *ever* again."

Oh, boy. This is going to take time we simply do not have. "Fine," I say loudly. "Leave him. We are out of here."

Poppy does a double take. "Are you suggesting—"

"In about ten seconds, this place is going to be swarming with guards," Izumi says.

"Let's *go*," urges Toby.

Charlotte strides to the cell exit. We follow. Owen Elliott leaps to his feet, eyes now fully open and wide with fear. "Don't leave me!" he howls.

"Well, then *hurry* up," Poppy admonishes.

But we've taken too long. Two guards materialize before us. One is bald with a creepy tattoo of a snake crawling up his neck. The other has thick eyebrows that meet in the middle of his forehead, like a caterpillar is napping on his face. Neither looks happy. Fortunately, I still have the sticky caramel-explosive-shoelace device in my palm.

"Get behind me!" I yell. As Snake and Caterpillar charge in, I hurl the caramel ball at the ground in front of them and shrink back. It lands in a small puddle, fizzles briefly, and dies. The guards stare at it.

"It doesn't work when it's *wet*," Toby whispers. This is absolutely a design flaw that must be addressed in exploding caramel 2.0. Now we're in serious trouble.

Caterpillar kicks the hunk of caramel out of the way. It sticks to the sole of his boot. He tries to work it off with the other boot, but it's all oozy, and that just makes things worse. He sits down hard and begins picking at the mess with a stray rock. Now the goo is on his hands. It migrates to his face, tangling in the woolly unibrow. His lips stick together. Toby watches, fascinated.

Snake, unaware of Caterpillar's sticky situation, yammers into his walkie-talkie, confident words like "we got them" and "no big deal." Adults. They always underestimate us. And this means we have a shot. I glance at Izumi and Charlotte, who offer a slight nod. I count down from three in my head and shout, "Hey, Snake!"

"Huh?" Snake never sees Izumi come at him from

the right, hitting him full-on. He tumbles to the ground. Caterpillar wants to help, but his hands are completely encapsulated in melted caramel. Charlotte swoops in, grabs the zip-tie cuffs, and secures Snake before he even knows what happened.

"Get his feet!" I yell. Izumi swipes the length of rope from Snake's belt and binds his feet. He curses a lot. Toby stuffs a stray glove in his mouth. It can't taste good. Quickly, we cuff Caterpillar, although that seems like over-kill. He is a mess. We run.

Well, most of us do. It takes a second to realize that Owen Elliott is frozen in place, staring at Snake and Caterpillar. Charlotte is right about the zombie apocalypse. Owen Elliott will be eaten first.

I sprint back into the cell. "Come on!" I get behind him and give him a shove.

"But you just, like, *assaulted* that guard."

"It's nothing permanent."

"But . . ."

"Can we talk about this later?" I plead. Finally, he starts to move, but sluggishly, as if running is optional. It's not. When Veronica wanted to motivate me, she somehow managed to make me want the same thing she did. But I'm not as good as Veronica, so I settle for blunt.

"If you don't hurry up," I hiss, "you will become a permanent part of this lava tube system. In two hundred years, archaeologists will uncover your bones and wonder why you didn't run faster."

His expression is shocked, but at least his feet start to move.

We catch up with the others. Izumi leads. The tunnel grows tighter. I hear the rushing water before I see it, the sound of thousands of gallons tumbling by very quickly. A torrent. I glance at Poppy. Her face is barely visible in the poor lighting of the tunnel, but I can tell this is not what she expected.

"That's a river," Charlotte says.

"A big one," adds Izumi.

"Isn't this supposed to be the way out?" asks Toby.

Poppy closes her eyes. "I thought it would be . . . smaller."

"Oh, this just keeps getting worse," Owen Elliott says with a moan.

"Is there another way out?" I ask.

Poppy shrugs. "No way to know."

"What if we, you know, jump in the river?" asks Izumi. "Where do we end up?"

"Dead?" suggests Toby.

"In the ocean," Charlotte says. "But look, there's light that way, so it can't be that far. And hopefully we pop out close to a beach. I mean, if the dead thing doesn't happen."

"Hopefully?" Izumi asks.

Footsteps echo in the distance. The guards close in. "Here's what I'm thinking," says Toby calmly. "I'm *not* getting caught by a bunch of lunatics. I'm not going through what we went through with Zachary Hazard again. No way. Not ever." His eyes are steely, determined.

Charlotte and Izumi nod solemnly in agreement. And with that, the three of them hold hands and jump into the raging underground river, vanishing before I eek out a scream for them to stop.

Poppy watches the spot where they disappeared. "I don't know who Zachary Hazard is," she says, "but I'm not hanging around here waiting for those guards. They do not have good intentions." With a little wave at a startled Owen Elliott, she takes the plunge, gone in an instant.

Owen Elliott, mouth frozen in a little O, cautiously backs away from the edge. "I am *not* jumping in there," he says. "You guys are crazy."

"It won't be so bad," I lie. "Kind of like those water park rides."

"Except in those rides you have a *boat*." Owen's eyeballs

look fit to pop out of his skull. But it's about to get worse.

Snake steps out of the gloom behind us. He clenches his fists and grins wildly. "Let's see you escape now," he snarls. "You're trapped! Think you're so smart, do you?"

I grab Owen Elliott by the wrist. He resists. I'm going to have to pull him in. Can he even swim? The guard takes advantage of the split-second hesitation and lunges for Owen, getting a handful of his ugly Hawaiian shirt. I yank him toward me, but the guard is bigger and stronger. And I have no more tricks up my sleeve or on my spy phone. But I do *have* the spy phone.

With as much precision as I can muster, I hurl the gold spy phone at Snake's head. It hits him right above the eye, hard enough to draw blood. He howls, releasing his grip on Owen Elliott. And that's all I need.

We spill over the edge into the river.

Chapter 34

A BIG MISTAKE.

THIS IS WHAT IT MUST FEEL LIKE to ride the spin cycle in a washing machine. I can't tell up from down. I lose my grip on Owen Elliott almost immediately, but I know he's close, as he kicks me in the face a number of times while we tumble along with the rushing water. I bounce off the steep, rocky sides of the river, leaving a layer of skin behind. The brackish water stings and burns my eyes. It's so completely dark. This might be the end. I never would have guessed it would be like *this*.

After what seems like an eternity but is probably only fifteen seconds, the water flattens out. The rushing waves calm. The light in the distance grows brighter. Owen Elliott floats on his back a few feet from me. I elbow him just to make sure he's alive. He shoots me a dirty look. Confirmation. I tread water as the current pushes us along.

From the mouth of the tunnel, we drop about five feet into the gentle ocean. The full moon lights up a white sand beach a brief swim away. Four waterlogged bodies lie on the water's edge.

"This way," I gurgle, nudging Owen Elliott toward shore.

"I'm going to die," he says, matter-of-fact.

"If that was going to happen," I say, "it would have already."

"Do you always have this much fun?" he asks.

"I try." He grimaces but paddles along until we drag ourselves up on the sand and collapse.

It's a full ten minutes before anyone says a word. We've had a number of near-death experiences, but this one felt dramatic. Perhaps because much of it happened underwater. I'm pleased no one is actively crying.

Charlotte groans and rolls toward me. "That might have been the worst idea ever."

"You'll have to be more specific," replies Izumi.

"But we made it," Poppy points out.

"Barely," adds Toby.

Oh, no. Toby. The gold spy phone. Is now the time to confess? I decide to wait. It's been a long twenty-four hours. We lie on the sand until the moon sinks and a bright orange sun creeps up over the horizon. Day.

"As soon as we find a dry phone," I croak, "I'm going to call Jennifer and yell at her."

Izumi rubs her temples. "I can't think until I have food," she groans.

"I hate to point this out to you," I say, "but we have the clothes on our backs. And just barely. We can't afford breakfast."

"Not so fast," says Toby. He removes his shoe, dumping out the accumulated mud, sand, water, and a few startled little fish. He peels back the inner foot bed, producing two soggy twenty-dollar bills.

"Sometimes old technology is best," he says. "Breakfast is on me."

We end up at a small roadside shack that sells Belgian waffles, piled high with chunks of pineapple and topped with syrup and whipped cream. The lady behind the counter, her hair tied up in an orange bandanna, barely bats an eye when we roll up, which makes me wonder what sorts of people frequent her waffle stand.

Sitting on a long bench, no one speaks as we cram food

into our mouths, except for the occasional *mmmm*. The sun warms our shoulders, drying our clothes, stiff with salt water. My eyelids are crusty. I'm exhausted but exhilarated. We've managed to keep the Ghost from getting what he wanted for long enough to get help. I wonder if he's even here. I'd love to see him marched out of those creepy lava tubes in handcuffs.

Izumi zeroes in on the one remaining pineapple chunk on my paper plate. "Are you going to eat that?" I dutifully hand it over and ask them what happened on the plane.

"They took our backpacks, right off the bat," Charlotte says. "When they didn't find what they were looking for, they threatened to bring in someone to make us talk. Or sing. Yeah. I think they said 'sing.' Clichéd bad guys are the worst."

"Sing about Blackout?" I ask.

"I think so," says Toby. "They seemed to think we knew all about what they wanted. How did you find us, anyway?

"Magic fabric sewn into Owen's shirt," I say.

"It's not *magic*," Poppy says. "It's *smart*."

"You mean the shirt Owen puked on?" asks Charlotte. "That added some excitement to the journey." It also explains the ugly Hawaiian shirt. I glance at him, but he stares at his uneaten waffle, unlike Toby, who is busy licking the last bits of whipped cream from his plate.

"What?" Toby asks.

"You have whipped cream on your nose." Toby crosses his eyes to see it and licks it away. How does he do that?

"Gross," says Izumi.

"You're just jealous," he responds.

"No," she says. "I'm really not."

"Do you think they'd let us stay here for a short vacation?" Charlotte asks. "I mean, if we've really uncovered the Ghost's headquarters, shouldn't we get *something* out of the deal?"

Birds chirp. Palm trees sway in the breeze. The air is sweet. We've escaped the evil underground lair. We didn't drown. So when Owen Elliott, who has not said a word since crawling out on the sand, flips out, it is both surprising and not.

"They wanted to kill us!" he yells, overturning his plate. His waffle lands in the dirt. "We might have been *tortured*."

"I don't think it was 'might,'" Charlotte interrupts. "I think it was definite."

Owen Elliott's cheeks flare red, and it's not from the building heat. "What if they pulled out my fingernails? Or my teeth?"

"You watch too many movies," Izumi comments. "More likely they would have forced us to watch nonstop cat videos until we confessed."

Charlotte giggles. Toby meows. Owen Elliott does not approve of the hilarity.

"You sit here and *joke*!" he cries. "Like what happened is no big deal. We were *kidnapped*. We were *threatened*. We were . . ." He gulps the air like a fish out of water.

"Breathe," suggests Izumi. But he's not done.

"I was all alone! And do you know what they said? Do you? They said they had found a way to remotely *kill* people by delivering poison through their *phone*. They just need to be *holding* it. Or have it in their pocket. And no one would ever know why they were dead! They were going to test it on us. They thought that was so *funny*. And you guys, you sit here and . . . and . . ." He sputters, his fury depleted, shoulders sagging.

Silence. All eyes are on Owen Elliott. My mind races in circles, chasing its tail. Finally, Toby speaks up. "Did you say 'poison'?"

 Chapter 35

BACK FOR ROUND TWO.

THIS IS BAD. Very bad. The worst. I glance at Izumi, who looks at Charlotte, who stares at Toby, who eyeballs me. My heart pounds through the stiff, dry fabric of my Smith T-shirt. The waffles, delicious just moments ago, roil my stomach.

"Now, Owen Elliott," I say quietly, "tell us exactly what they said in the cave. Did they really say 'poison'?"

He's exasperated, pulling at tufts of his salt-crunchy hair. "Yes! They went on and on about fear and how that is all you need to control people and if you can find a way to make them afraid they will accept things they never would otherwise."

"They aren't after Poppy's Blackout," I say. "They are after—"

"Cookies," Toby whispers, his face pale. "They want a way to poison people with the touch of a button."

A stunned silence settles in. "They wanted *us* all along," I say. "Can they *do* it? Would it *work*?"

Toby nods his head gravely. "Yeah. It will work." Well, that's just great. "And it explains why they were so thrilled to find *our* phones after they kidnapped us. And so angry when they realized the app wasn't on them. It's only on the gold one."

Sometimes I experience a jolt, like a shock to my brain, when the odds suddenly shift and are no longer in my favor. Toby sees it on my face and visibly blanches.

"You. Did. Not."

I fight to keep from gagging on waffle. "I had no choice!" I blurt. "That phone saved our lives!" I skip the part about how I used it as a brick, hurling it at Snake's head. "And besides, you gave it to me. Why was the Cookie app on there to begin with?"

"Because you kept breaking all the regular spy phones!" Toby shouts. "That was my beta! That's where I *test* things!" Toby rarely raises his voice, so this throws me back on my heels.

"Wait a minute," says Charlotte. "Just to clarify, you gave *cookies* to the bad guys?"

Great. She picks now to pile on. "It was an accident!"

"Abby is notorious for losing spy gear," Izumi explains to Poppy and Owen Elliott, whose eyes bounce from me to Toby and back to me again. "It's a problem."

I throw my hands in the air. "I didn't do it on purpose!"

"You never do!" shouts Toby.

Charlotte stomps her foot. This gets our attention. "Enough," she says. "Silence. Toby, can they get what they need off Abby's phone?"

"Yes," Toby says, simmering.

I stand abruptly, my empty plate sticky with syrup falling to my feet. "We need that phone back," I say.

Izumi jumps up next to me. "Before they can steal cookies," she says.

"I guess we're going back to the Ghost's lair?" asks Charlotte. Does she seem hopeful? Hasn't she had enough?

Poppy chokes on her tongue. "Are you guys *insane*?"

Maybe. But every second counts. We cannot let the Ghost's people extract what he needs from the spy phone.

"Toby. Owen Elliott. Poppy," I say. "Find a working phone. Call my mother. Tell her to *hurry*."

"And where will you be going exactly?" asks Poppy, squinting into the sun.

"We're going after that phone," I say.

"You're aware you have nothing?" Toby points out. "No spy gear. Zippo."

I am *keenly* aware. But sometimes a girl just has to rely on her wits. Emma and Gemma Glass would be so proud. "We'll be fine," I say.

"I hate when she says that," Izumi mutters. "It's never true. It's always the opposite." But then she smiles, a big broad grin. And Charlotte smiles too. And we start to laugh, well aware that Owen Elliott and Poppy watch us with dismay. The laughter crescendoes, until my eyes leak tears, leaving little trails down my salty cheeks. I heave with convulsive hiccups.

"Don't mind them," Toby says with a dismissive wave. "This is just how they roll."

And it is. No matter the odds, no matter how daunting or scary or downright stupid, as long as I have my friends with me, I'm not afraid.

"I totally love you guys," I whisper through the hiccups. Izumi slaps me so hard on the back, my teeth almost fly out of my head. That's what I get for declarations of love. But the hiccups are gone.

"Works every time," she says as I catch my breath.

"When you get down in the tubes," Toby says, his face serious, "look for a server room, someplace with tons of computers. They will want to amplify the Cookie app and push it everywhere as soon as they can."

"Lots of computers," I say. "Got it."

"And if it's already been loaded onto the servers," he says grimly, "you're going to have to kill it."

"How do I do that?" I ask, suddenly a little queasy.

"Don't move," he says, dashing to the waffle lady. He returns with a pen. "Hold out your arm." Quickly, he writes several strings of code from my wrist to my elbow. Don't get it wet. Enter it *exactly* like this."

"Okay. Let's regroup in that little town we went through on the bus. Remember, Poppy? There were gardens."

"That narrows it down," she says, but she does not argue or offer me a different plan.

"Find it," I say. "And be careful. They are bound to be looking for us. We will meet you there. Hopefully soon."

"And if you don't?" Owen Elliott asks, just this side of hysterical.

"We *will*," I say.

All other options are simply unacceptable.

Chapter 36

SECOND TIME IS THE CHARM.

WITH THE SPARE CHANGE from the waffles, we catch the same bus Poppy and I rode earlier to the stop nearest to the Ghost's fancy empty plantation. It's even the same bus driver. She does a double take when she sees us, but it's not because she recognizes us. It's more like horror at our condition. We've looked better. I'm proud of Charlotte for not demanding we spend our last dollar on a tube of ChapStick. That's bravery for you.

We have the element of surprise going for us. They won't expect a return visit after we tried so hard to escape. That would be ludicrous. And foolhardy. And unwise. Illogical, even. And, possibly, stupid.

Instead of plotting how we get back into the Ghost's hideaway and steal back the spy phone, Charlotte and Izumi want to know what is so special about Poppy. "Why was her name on that paper?"

"She's a really good planner," I say. "As in her plans have more than step number one. And she thinks about contingencies. For real."

The girls look appropriately impressed. "So she's like Mrs. Smith to Jennifer?" asks Izumi.

"Exactly."

"Interesting," says Izumi.

"You're not going to ditch us to partner up with Poppy, are you?" asks Charlotte, her gaze intense.

"What? No! Never. Ugh. Don't even joke about that. She was freaking out from the first minute. The only time she was calm was when she was planning. Or blowing things up. She liked that part too."

"Had to check," Charlotte says with a wink.

The bus rolls to the dirt shoulder and we disembark. Izumi and Charlotte follow me into the edge of the abandoned coffee field. I plunge into the tall weeds, and the girls follow without a word.

Soon, the grand plantation house comes into view. "It's empty?" asks Charlotte.

"Like a movie set or something," I say.

"They blindfolded us until we were down in the lava tubes," Izumi adds. "We didn't see anything. It was not okay."

It strikes me that my friends have been through a lot in the past couple of years and might be the bravest people I know. I have to remember to tell them that later, when we are not on the verge of adding to the list.

"The lava tube entrance is this way," I say. "Follow me."

Because we don't have any spy gadgets and the dog-whisperer skills are hit or miss, we give the house a wide berth and stay hidden in the brush. But it was dark when Poppy fell through the crack in the earth, and it takes me a while to find it.

Izumi and Charlotte are patient, following me around in circles. "Do you think anyone has noticed we're not back yet?" asks Izumi.

"Doubtful," says Charlotte. "They think we're busy with the wits task."

"I wonder who will win the Challenge?"

"Not us."

"Is Poppy really a dog whisperer?" asks Izumi.

"Kind of," I say. "Here it is." I stand over the fissure in the earth. It looks no less welcoming in the light of day.

Why didn't I just throw a rock at Snake's head? *Why* did I throw the phone?

"It's volcanic," says Izumi, pushing at the ground with her toe. "This whole island is cracking and splitting all the time. I guess we crawl down there and find the phone."

"Which is where?" asks Charlotte.

Good question.

"The last time," I say, "Poppy and I went right. We know there are no giant server rooms that way. So this time we go left." My friends agree this sounds perfectly reasonable. I spend another few seconds staring down the hole before Charlotte nudges me.

"Are you going or what?" she asks.

"On it," I say. "When you drop, tuck tight so you don't hurt yourselves. And be careful."

Izumi snorts with laughter. "Be careful. That's a good one!"

"By the way," Charlotte asks, "how do we get out again?"

"The river?" Izumi suggests.

"Or maybe the main ladder," I say. "If we're patient, and don't get caught. That might work."

"Speaking of getting caught," Izumi cautions, "we should probably stop talking."

We move through the tube as silently as possible.

Voices echo, but it's hard to pinpoint their location with all this rock. They could be right behind us or miles away. It's creepy. I push it from my mind. Freaking out for no good reason is self-indulgent when I'm sure there will be opportunities to freak out for good reasons very soon.

We walk for a long time. Only once do we come close to colliding with a man and a woman standing in a wide section of the tube. The man is tall and has to hunch over to avoid conking his head. They don't look evil. They look ordinary. Do they have any idea what the Ghost is capable of if we don't stop him? How can they stand there engaged in casual conversation? We slip by, grateful for the shadows.

The rocky corridors twist and turn and randomly branch off. We might be going in circles. For morale's sake, I keep this to myself, until up ahead we see bright lights coming from a tube. Beethoven's Ninth Symphony drifts out and fills the air. Guarding the entrance are our old friends Caterpillar and Snake. Caterpillar has cleaned himself up, although he now has a bald spot in his eyebrow.

"Really?" I mutter. "These two again?" We huddle some distance away in a dark pocket against the rock. The guards wear neutral expressions and stare into space as good guards should.

"Do you smell that?" Izumi asks, sniffing the air. "It's warm, like electric, staticky, you know?" I nod even though all I smell is wet rock. "It comes from running a lot of computers at once."

Right, which means we have to get past the guards. Again.

"Maybe we just politely ask them to step aside," suggests Charlotte.

"Oh, yeah. I bet that will work," Izumi says with a laugh.

A plan starts to come together in my mind. It might not work. Who am I kidding? It's almost guaranteed to fail. But unless we do something fast, the world will be in serious trouble.

Chapter 37

GIVE AS GOOD AS YOU GET.

CHARLOTTE PULLS HER HAIR BACK into a tight ponytail. Izumi uses the edge of her filthy T-shirt to wipe off her face. "How do we look? Will they recognize us?"

"You look beautiful," I say. And I totally mean it. "Like, invincible. Fierce."

"Don't get carried away," Izumi says.

"Wish us luck," Charlotte adds.

We do a quick group hug, and I get a whiff of salt water. I wonder if, in the future, every time I smell the ocean I will come right back to this moment? That would be okay. Nothing has gone off the rails yet.

The plan is for Charlotte and Izumi to distract and

disable the guards. Meanwhile, I race down the lava tube, grab the phone, and we escape. Explaining my idea, I feel a twinge, and after a moment, I recognize that I miss Poppy and her plans. How did *that* happen?

Charlotte takes a deep inhale, slowly lets the air out through her nose. "Let's do this," she says. Izumi loops an arm around Charlotte's neck and they stagger into the light. Charlotte drags Izumi, screaming.

"My friend is injured! Oh, please help us! We fell through a hole in the ground! I think I'm going to faint!" Now Izumi starts screaming, as if blind with pain. The girls keep their backs to the guards, who rush over, unable to ignore the noise. The screaming is outrageous, echoing off the walls, amplified by stone. When Snake leans over to get a better look at Izumi's face, he gets a quick elbow to the bridge of the nose. I hear the *crack*. That's got to smart. Charlotte rests both hands on Caterpillar's shoulders and drives her knee into his guts. He goes down in a heap. Classic Veronica moves! She would be so proud. But there's no time to stand around and admire their work. I take off down the lava tube, tripping on the uneven floor and bouncing off the walls. Beethoven gets louder and louder until it feels like my brain is rattling around in my head. Finally, I arrive at the outer rim of an enormous room carved out of the lava, the inside of a hollowed-out mountain. Izumi was right. There are a lot of computers. Floor-to-ceiling storage cabinets line the rough rock walls, disappearing into the distant darkness. Fans spin to keep the servers from overheating despite the underground chill. A man in a white lab coat, probably the Ghost's most recent evil scientist, stands at a high table with several monitors, his back to me. He taps a keyboard, pauses to conduct a few bars of music, and returns to the keyboard. At his elbow is my gold spy phone, plugged into a deck of churning machines.

Don't worry, little spy phone! I'm here to save you!

Before I can iron out the specifics of how best to do that, the man at the monitors whirls around.

I *know* that face. I've *seen* that face. My entire body goes cold, and it's all I can do not to scream as his eyes bore into me.

Can it really be the Ghost? *Right here?*

He grins as if he's considering eating me. A hot bubble of panic rises in my chest. "Abigail Hunter herself," he hisses. He's not very tall, but his fingers are extra long and thin. He waves them in the air like tentacles. A shock of unruly white hair frames a surprisingly youthful face. For some reason, I expected jowls. "It *had* to be you, didn't it? Trying to get done what your mother could not. She came close. Many times. But your poor pathetic Center is simply not up to the task of stopping *me*."

My eyes drift to the phone. He grabs it up, yanking it free from the tangle of wires, and waves it at me. "You came for this, did you? Foolish girl. In five minutes, that beautiful code will be surfing my digital ocean, enabling me to terrify the world into submission." His eyes are frantic, like he pulled an all-nighter to study for an exam but might fail anyway. "The one thing I've learned in life is that it's easier to be feared than to be loved. A big, scary weapon isn't necessary to control people. You just need their dismay, their distress, their anxiety. A poisoning here and there, so random, so unpredictable, they will see malevolence behind every corner, under every rock. They will never suspect their *devices*. And even if they did, most would be loath to give them up. Addicts! Of course, when I sail in, offering to save them, they will give me what I want. Whatever it is. Who knew taking over the world could be so *easy*?"

My feet are glued to the floor. "It won't work," I croak.

"Oh, but it will," he scoffs. "Do you really think you and your band of insignificant mischief makers can actually stop me?"

"Yes?"

"I admire your confidence, misplaced as it may be,"

he says, circling me, studying me. I'm frozen in place, my mind blank. "Say, I have an idea. Why don't you come work for *me*?" He snickers. "You know Lola Smith is never going to let you in that school you care so much about. But if you join my team, I will actually let you *play*. You'll get the glory you so badly want."

This snaps me out of my trance. Is he really offering me a spot on his evil bad-guy team? That takes some nerve. "No thank you," I say politely. "I'd rather eat glass."

"It figures," he says. "You're all caught up in good and bad, but really there is only power and who has it. And you kids don't. You can do only what *we* allow you to do."

But that's not true. When we stick together we can do anything. "You're wrong," I say.

He flashes a wicked grin. "How delightfully naive. Maybe you'd like to see a demonstration of the power I'm talking about? Hmmm, whom shall we target first? How about half the travelers in Heathrow? Or all the drivers stuck in traffic in Los Angeles? Or maybe the Smith School volleyball team?" He laughs, a terrible sound that reverberates around the cave. I want to cover my ears. "This is going to be diabolically *fun*."

Fun is a roller coaster, fun is riding a bike with no hands, fun is *not* being randomly poisoned by a madman. He waves the phone around like a conductor's baton, clutching it tightly as the music soars. And that gives me an idea.

It's risky. Poppy would be horrified, and it probably won't work, but I'm willing to take a chance. I step closer. I have to be within range for the phone to hear my voice. "Fun?" I say with a snicker. "What do you know about fun? You live all alone in a *cave*."

The Ghost stops short. "I do *not* live all alone," he says, pointing at me with the phone. "I have an army of people at my beck and call."

"That's not the same as having friends," I say, inching forward.

The Ghost's face goes red, in stark contrast to his shock of wild white hair. "Stop talking right now."

"Did you know loneliness can shorten your life span? It's actually bad for you. I read that someplace. Probably in school."

He has gone full tomato face. Little bits of spit fly from his mouth. "I told you to be *quiet*." But I'm almost there. One more step should do it. Please let me be close enough. Please let this work.

"I'm bad at following directions," I say. "Ask anyone."

"You insolent little brat!" he cries.

"Veronica! Horn! Bees! Lightning! Snarling dog! Cookies!" I shout. As all the apps struggle to launch at once, the phone becomes red hot in the Ghost's hand. He screams and tries to throw it, but it adheres to his skin. This is my moment. I summon my best Deadhead the Rose, planting my foot and exploding my other leg in a roundhouse kick to the back of the Ghost's head. He flies forward, the phone still glowing with heat in his hand, hits his head on the cave wall, and crumples in a heap.

Adrenaline surging through my veins, I watch for movement, signs that he is not done. But he's completely out, eyes closed, face slack, chest rising and falling with each shallow breath.

"Spy phone off," I say. Wobbly and light-headed, I stand over him. The phone smolders in his hand, slowly cooling from red to orange back to tarnished gold. Sometimes our flaws turn out to be our strengths, but I still think Toby needs to fix this problem in the next version.

I nudge the Ghost with my toe. What happened to him? Who turned him into this monster? Did he want something so badly that he would compromise everything for it? No prize is worth trading your soul. When he wakes up, he will be in a world of pain.

So not my problem.

Chapter 38

ARE WE HAVING FUN YET?

I GINGERLY STEP over the Ghost's inert body, a little skittish, convinced he will rear up again any second like the bad guys always do in the movies. But he just lies there as if having a nap on the cold, hard floor.

Quickly, I find the command screen on the mainframe and begin to type out the sequence. But my arm is wet, and the last number runs like a little black river to my wrist.

"No. No. No!" Is it a seven or a one? I want to cry. But this is the reason I'm out here and Poppy is behind the desk, just like Jennifer and Mrs. Smith. I tap the seven, hit enter, and hold my breath. The servers churn and hum. *Program Deleted* appears on the screen.

"Yes!" From the Ghost's desk, I swipe an empty coffee mug, peel the spy phone from his grip, and deposit it, still hot, into the mug. It won't be long until someone realizes what's happened. It's time to go. Without a glance back at my nemesis and my mother's before me, I sprint from the room. Izumi and Charlotte run in my direction. "Did you do it?" Izumi asks, breathless.

I hold up the fried phone. "Yeah. Done. Let's get out of here." We charge through the tunnel, back the way we came, skirting around the incapacitated guards and toward the main ladder to freedom. And everything is going so well! We're going to make it!

Until suddenly, it's not and we aren't.

Four guards, shoulder to shoulder, block access to the precious ladder. More guards? How much security does the Ghost have down here, anyway?

"Not so fast," barks a guard. They don't look willing to negotiate. Besides, we have nothing to offer, other than the charred remains of what was once a very cool spy phone.

"We could fight our way out," Izumi whispers.

"Not great odds," I reply.

"Ugh," says Charlotte. "This is taking too long. I really want a shower. Thoughts?"

I have a lot of thoughts. None of them are productive.

But just when I think there is no hope, things take a turn for the weird. A pair of black stilettos appears on the ladder, followed by black pants, a black shirt, and a black leather jacket. *Tinker Bell?*

"Is that who I think it is?" whispers Izumi.

"Yup."

"Did we figure out if she is on the side of good or evil?"

"She is on the side of Tinker Bell," I say.

"Great."

Tinker Bell hops from the ladder and dusts off her hands. She glances around, eyebrow arched. I don't think she approves of the decorating. Several of her henchmen descend from above. Her gaze lands on me. She smiles. "It is *so* nice to see you again, Abigail," she squeaks.

Keenly aware that we are trapped down here, I offer a half smile, mostly to hide my panic, and wait to see what will happen next.

Tinker does a slow spin. "This is the Ghost's top secret brand-new international headquarters? Dreary. Could use some color. And maybe some sunlight. Does he only hire vampires?" She snorts at her joke. The henchmen chuckle. I bet they are paid to do that. "I have to say I expected . . . more. But I'm not here for a vacation. What did you do with the man himself?" She zeroes in on me. "Because I know you did something."

"I . . . um . . . deadheaded the rose," I stutter. "But it's temporary. I think so, anyway."

Tinker waves me off. "Kids. Do you ever make sense? I'm not even going to pretend I know what you're talking about. Regardless, this is the *best*. So many secrets here, mine for the taking." She snaps her fingers. "Boys, secure the facility."

As more of her posse descend the ladder, the ones on the ground move forward, plowing under the Ghost's people, who are about as surprised as we are. It's a coup.

We step out of the way, backs pressed against the cold rock wall. I smell Tinker Bell's citrusy perfume. Her red lipstick is perfect, no smudges. She wedges her sunglasses deep into her mountain of hair and returns her attention to us. Lifting my chin with a manicured finger, she forces me to look right at her. She's not medusa—I won't be turned to actual stone or anything, but it sure feels dangerous.

"You did good," Tinker says. "Of course, I'd have preferred you didn't wreck my car and beat up my driver, but I'm willing to overlook those things because you led me *right* where I wanted to go."

"Were you following us the whole time?" I whisper. Her gaze is too intense. I shiver.

"Trade secrets, my dear. You aspiring spy types could learn a thing or two from our side." Her lips twitch into a frightening smile. "But for now, you look a mess. I suggest you get out of here. Perhaps consider bathing."

She doesn't have to ask twice. Sometimes the best thing a girl can hope for is to escape and live to fight another day.

We inch around her toward the ladder. "And remember, ladies"—Tinker Bell cackles—"there's a new sheriff in town!"

Chapter 39

THE SMITH SCHOOL FOR CHILDREN.

THERE ARE SO MANY THINGS I could be getting in trouble for I can't keep track. Losing the Challenge for Smith, causing Team OP to lose the Challenge for Smith, going AWOL, illegal flying, conspiring with a known black hat, leading one notorious bad person into the secret lair of another notorious bad person, using unapproved spy gear, losing unapproved spy gear, risking life and limb—my own and others'—disobeying my mother, who was not happy finding us in Hawaii and having to explain to Mrs. Smith why we were there, and swapping the required Smith School uniform for shorts and a T-shirt while at Briar.

We will not get credit for saving the integrity of the

Challenge or neutralizing the Ghost, and I know better than to ask for it. I try to quiet my mind as I cross campus, but there's a lot to think about. For starters, how do I pay back Iceman? She's unhappy the Cookie app will not be forthcoming, and I really don't want her mad at me. And what happened to Baldy and Jane Ann? My mother mentioned an island off Alaska but did not offer details. But all that will have to wait until after my date with destiny, or Mrs. Smith, as it were.

Just as I'm about to pull open the doors to Main Hall, Owen Elliott races up, breathless. I haven't seen him much since we got back. He's avoiding me, and I'm unsure how that makes me feel.

"Abby," he gasps. "I'm glad I caught you. Is this the Mrs. Smith meeting?" Everyone on campus is waiting to see what will happen. The daughter of the former headmaster is in serious trouble. They don't know the details, of course, but they smell blood in the water. Boarding school can be boring. We latch on to whatever drama we can.

"Yeah," I say, belying my pounding heart. "No big deal." But it is. I don't want Smith to be over for me. I'm not ready.

"I just wanted to wish you good luck," Owen Elliott says, a bloom of heat rising on his cheeks, "and to say that I really hope it . . . um . . . works out and stuff. And if

you end up, you know, staying, we can be, well, friends."
He runs his fingers through his hair, stalling. "What I
mean is I like you, but I can't, you know, *like* you. You're
too . . . complicated . . . and a little dangerous . . . and kind
of scary. . . ."

I hold up a hand for him to stop. Message received.
Oddly, my heart slows to normal. If someone is going to
like me, they have to like all the parts, the sharp points,
the rough edges, the smooth lines, because I'm not chang-
ing those. Besides, I never claimed to be *ordinary*. "You
don't have to explain," I say. "I gotta go."

I feel his eyes on me as I walk toward Mrs. Smith's
office, but I don't look back. The headmaster waits outside
her door, ushering me in without a word. I keep my face
neutral. My uniform is wrinkled beyond hope, the horrible
red tie hanging limp around my neck.

"Abigail," Mrs. Smith says, closing the door. "*Why* do
we keep finding ourselves in this situation?" When I begin
to sputter a reply, she cuts me off. "The answer is you are
allergic to rules. You cannot follow them. You think they
don't apply to you."

That's not true. It's just that sometimes they get in
the way.

"To make matters worse," she continues, "the mediocre

Taft team won the Challenge. And you know how I feel about them. I'm *not* happy. Poppy was meant to win, but you were too busy leading her on a wild-goose chase across the Pacific Ocean. That girl is going places. You'd be wise to pay attention."

I anticipated a lot of this, but corrupting Poppy was not even on the radar. The words *I'm sorry* sit on the tip of my tongue but refuse to budge. I just can't spit them out. Because I guess I'm not really sorry.

Mrs. Smith studies a portrait of the fourth head-master, James Smith III, that hangs on the wall. She stares at him for a long time. My wool skirt is so itchy I want to scream, but I remain completely still. There is no way I'll give her the pleasure of anxious fidgeting.

"While I recommended immediate expulsion," she says, without looking at me, "others have intervened on your behalf. It seems your stunt cut the Ghost off at the knees." Was Tinker Bell long gone with all of the Ghost's secrets by the time the Center showed up in Hawaii? No one has mentioned her, so I haven't either. I just don't see it helping my situation.

I hold my breath, waiting for my punishment to come down from on high. I bet I'm looking at kitchen duty for the rest of my life. I'll be up to my elbows in burned macaroni and cheese until I'm one hundred years old.

Mrs. Smith clears her throat, turns her gaze in my direction. "Instead," she says, "the Center has decided to admit you into the spy training program."

Did she just say what I think she said? My head almost explodes. My ears ring. "Can you say that again, please?"

She grits her teeth as if the words taste foul. "Spy program. Here. You."

My vision blurs. I might faint. I *am* exceptional enough! "Yes!" I blurt. "We're in! We're *in*!"

Mrs. Smith gives me an icy smile, and that's when I know my glory will be fleeting, that her revenge will be something much worse than burned macaroni and cheese.

"We? Oh, my dear, I think you misunderstand me. You will be part of a team with Poppy Parsons. Just the *two* of you. None of the others. Sorry."

She watches me like a hawk as my insides drop. This was her plan: to put me in an impossible situation and force my hand. But how bad would it be? Me and Poppy? I mean, we managed pretty well in Hawaii. She's completely annoying, of course, but our strengths are complementary. It could work.

But an image of the Ghost floats up in my memory. He said I could join his band of evil doers and get the glory.

But I don't *want* glory. Somewhere along the way spy school became an end unto itself. I forgot the reason I wanted it in the first place, and that is to make a better world. And there is more than one way to do that: just ask Gemma and Emma Glass. My heart steels itself for what I have to do next.

"Thank you for the offer," I say politely. "I appreciate the opportunity. But I already have a *team*. Izumi, Charlotte, and Toby? They are the best part of my life. So while I know I could do amazing things for the Center—I have, after all, saved the world a few times *already*—I decline the offer."

The words stick in my throat. Tears well in my eyes. Mrs. Smith smiles slowly, coldly.

"I suppose I will have to find Poppy a different, more willing partner," she says. "How unfortunate."

But is it? I have friends who get my jokes, who prop me up when I need it. I have friends who listen and laugh and understand me. My mother is *right*. I am loyal, determined, and fearless, and I do not quit. Especially when things get tough. *That's* what makes me exceptional. I know that now, and I would not trade it, or them, for anything in the world. There will be another chance, another opportunity, and when it rolls around, we will be ready.

I'm not unfortunate. I might just be the luckiest girl in the world.

Izumi, Charlotte, and Toby wait in the hallway, nervously pacing the shiny wooden floor.

"What happened?" Izumi whispers.

"Did she, you know, kick you out?" asks Toby, forehead wrinkled.

"Nah," I say. "She just lectured me. Are we surprised?"

My friends collectively exhale. "I'm so relieved," says Charlotte. "I really thought this might be it."

"No way," I say. "You guys are stuck with me."

We loop arms and head toward the Annex, chattering about cheese fries and how Toby got a weird message from Iceman, something about paying a debt. *Uh-oh.* Before I can explain, my phone rings. Jennifer. The last time I saw her she was rolling her eyes while Mrs. Smith yelled at her. "Well, that was certainly an exciting trip," she begins. "I was glad to be back on land. Alas, it did not last." In the background is boisterous singing.

"Are you *back* with the pirates?" I ask.

"Let's just say we had some unfinished business. I'm hoping it goes quickly. I'm not a big fan of the ocean." The sound of smashing glass interrupts, and Jennifer starts yelling in a language that might be pirate.

Suddenly, my chest seizes with the desire to tell her everything about Mrs. Smith, about how spy school is never going to happen for me, how I let her down. But my friends can't know the truth. I quickly swallow down the urge.

"That's nice," I squeak.

"Abigail," she says. "Now listen carefully. I know what just happened, and I know you probably can't talk about it." Seriously. How does she do that? "But I'm proud of you for so many things—for making the right choice, for not abandoning your friends, for being brave when you didn't have to be."

"But I . . ."

"No 'buts.' Everything is excellent. Well, except the pirates. They are still a pain. Anyway, I have an idea that I floated to the bosses back in Washington. They seemed to like it. I call it Spy School 2.0. What do you think?"

What do I *think*? I turn to my friends, who are watching me intently.

And I smile.

Acknowledgments

Writing a series is like hanging out with a best friend who sometimes totally gets on your nerves. It's been several months since I finished *Double Cross*, and I miss those kids, but I'm glad they are out there somewhere, always.

As always, a big thank-you to Leigh Feldman of Leigh Feldman Literary for guiding me through the choppy waters of publishing with a steady hand and nerves of steel. I'm grateful every day that you are on my team.

This is my third book with the extraordinary Alyson Heller. Her editorial insights are like emergency lighting on an airplane, leading me to where I need to go. The first time we met in person, we spent two hours talking about travel, and I knew right then we were going to be friends. And thank you to Vivienne To for book covers that capture exactly the essence of the series. I could not have imagined anything better. And to the entire team at Aladdin, thanks for making the process so easy.

Writers are solitary creatures, but there are always a handful of friends who keep us going when we just want to crawl back under the covers. Lisa Schmid, Eileen Rendahl, Christine Crawford, Linda Mellema—thank you.

And to my tween and teen kids, you have no idea how much I eavesdrop on your conversations and steal the good parts, do you? No, of course you don't, and thank goodness for that. Thank you for being who you are. The world needs you, now more than ever, and I know you are up to the challenge. You are my inspiration and my heart.

And finally this book is for Mike, my partner in everything that matters, because they all are.

**TURN THE PAGE FOR A SNEAK PEEK OF A
NEW ADVENTURE FROM BETH MCMULLEN!**

EIGHT MONTHS AGO—
PRAGUE, CZECH REPUBLIC

FROM THE OUTSIDE, MY LIFE PROBABLY LOOKS pretty good. I travel around the world with my archaeologist father searching for lost things. Not like misplaced keys or that library book you swear you returned. No, Professor Lawrence Benko is a *treasure hunter*. You know, Montezuma's gold or the plunder of the dreaded pirate Blackbeard. *That* kind of stuff. Last year we spent four months searching for the priceless Sword of Honjo Masamune, lost during World War II. The search turned out to be a wild-goose chase and a total bust. But every once in a while, the esteemed professor *finds* what he's looking for. That's when you read about him in the news or see him on television.

So what is traipsing around the world after my dad *really* like? Well, at twelve years old, I live out of a suitcase and have extra pages stapled into my passport because I used up the regular ones. I've been on all the continents except for Antarctica, and that is only because there are not many treasures buried in the ice. I've been to eleven schools in seven years, which means I know kids all over the world, but I have no *real* friends because who wants a friend who just ups and leaves at the drop of a hat? I learned to read on a boat traveling down the Mekong Delta and to divide fractions on an archaeological dig in Mali.

Dad says I'm a tinkerer. My current specialty is whirligig wind spinners made from tin cans, wire, and springs. The tinkering comes from having lots of idle time moving from place to place. When my father is in hot pursuit of some missing thing or another and 100 percent focused on his work, I am responsible for entertaining myself. I'm good at being alone. I barely even notice it. Not much, anyway.

For instance, right now I'm parked in a small dusty apartment that has been our home for thirteen hours. We came from Estonia and before that Bucharest. Or Istanbul? I can't remember. It all runs together. I'm staring out the window at two kids with backpacks down on the sidewalk. They are probably on their way to school. I notice them because one is laughing so hard at what the other just said, she doubles over to catch her breath. But I'm definitely *not* wondering what it would be like to have a friend who laughed at my jokes like that. No. I'm looking at the library across the street, so ornate and fancy it could be a royal palace. *That's* what I'm doing.

This morning, Dad took off to meet the archivist before the sun was even up, something urgent about old records and fairy tales. He left a note reminding me to do my homework before getting distracted by other projects. And while I appreciate his effort, this new whirligig I'm building is made from Coke cans and sparkles like a disco ball. It is *much* more interesting than equations or vocabulary lists. Also, when Dad goes into an archive or a library, he doesn't leave until they kick him out, which means I have plenty of time to do my homework before he gets back.

Except it turns out I don't. It's not even lunchtime when Dad crashes through the apartment's front door, hair wild and arms helicoptering. He's acting like he just got electrocuted. For the record, Dad and I look nothing alike. He's tall and lanky with silver hair and I'm short and solid with frizzy brown hair. His eyes are green like a cat and mine are brown like a mud puddle. Except Dad says they are flecked with gold and beautiful. Whatever.

"Lola!" Dad shouts, his eyes frantic. "Things have just taken a turn for the extraordinary!"

"They have?" I'm about to cut an important piece of Coke can, but I pause. When Dad is excited, the best solution is to wait him out. It never lasts more than three or four minutes. I put down my tin snips.

"Indeed." He's breathless, gulping at the air. "Places to go, people to see, things to do. Come on. Pack up. Time to move."

"But we *just* got here." This is a quick change of direction, even for us.

He waves me off. "I know. I know. But things are happening. Stupendous things. Unbelievable things."

Boy, he's really excited. "Stupendous" isn't an everyday word for Dad. "What are they?" I demand.

His expression falls flat. "I can't tell you." Great. Sometimes I can't get him to shut up about whatever artifact he's after and other times he's silent as the grave. Is it too much to ask for a happy medium?

"Then you shouldn't taunt me with 'stupendous' and 'unbelievable,'" I grumble.

Dad takes me by the shoulders. "I share your sorrow that we cannot stay longer in beautiful Prague, but I must take the tiger by the tail on this one. It requires a full-court press." Dad loves a good idiom, but I'm still annoyed.

Clearly he doesn't care, as he spins around the apartment, picking up the few things we've managed to unpack and hurling them into our bags. It occurs to me Dad has not asked about my homework and that is always his first question. Something strange is *definitely* going on.

"Fine. But I need an hour to take this apart." I point at the half-constructed whirligig. It's my most ambitious creation yet, and there is no way I'm going to mess it up because Dad is having some sort of unexplained melt-down. "Where are we going anyway?"

Dad eyes the three-foot whirligig with suspicion, as if seeing it for the first time. "Well, I'm headed to Budapest. But you are going to San Francisco."

I drop a coil of wire. "*Excuse* me? San Francisco?" Not that I don't like San Francisco. I love it there. I stay with Great-Aunt Irma, who is the best, and her companion gray parrot, Zeus, who's the best at being trouble. Irma always has three flavors of ice cream in the freezer and never nags me to brush my hair, although once Zeus tried to make a nest in there and I knew enough to take the hint. But the point is, Dad is dropping me like a hot potato. "Why?"

Dad flashes a pained expression. "Just for a few months."

"*Months?*"

"Weeks? Is that better? I can't say for sure, but it's a

necessary precaution," he explains. "It might not be safe."

"*What's* not safe?"

"Perhaps that's the wrong word? Well, in any case, not to worry. Everything is fine. It's just Irma would dearly love to see you and I figured now that it's almost summer, it would be a good time. Plus, I have things to do. They won't be fun for you. Very boring. Dull. Boring and dull."

"You *said* not safe."

"You misheard me. And the whirligig will have to stay."

I'm pretty good at being spontaneous. I mean, really. Look at me. But even I have my limits. "No. Way."

"You can't fly with it. It's very . . . weird." When I scowl at him, he retreats. "You know what I mean. They are picky about what you can bring on airplanes these days."

"I don't care. I'm not leaving it."

"You must."

"I refuse." I cross my arms against my chest defensively.

Dad's jaw tightens. In his head, he's reeling through strategies to get me to comply with his wishes. It won't work. He might as well give up now and save himself the time. I grimace, just in case my point is somehow unclear.

After glancing at his watch, he throws his hands up in the air. "Fine! I'll ship it to you."

I narrow my gaze. "You promise?"

"I swear."

"Pinkie swear?"

"I don't know what that is," he replies, perplexed.

"Never mind, a regular swear is fine, I guess. Just don't mess this up."

Dad looks at me, but really he's looking beyond me, seeing something in his mind's eye. A memory maybe or something to come. Whatever it is, it haunts him. "In this situation," he says gravely, "messing up is simply not an option."

Three hours later I'm on a plane to San Francisco.